ALCHEMY

The Tranquebar Book of Erotic Stories II

Sheba Karim's young adult novel, *Skunk Girl*, has been published in Denmark, India, Italy, Sweden and the United States. Her fiction has appeared in *580 Split*, *Asia Literary Review*, *Barn Owl Review*, *Femina*, *Kartika Review*, *Shenandoah*, *South Asian Review* and *Time Out Delhi*, as well as the anthologies *Electric Feather: The Tranquebar Book of Erotic Stories*, *Love Like That and Other Stories and Cornered: 14 Stories of Bullying and Defiance*. Two of her short stories have been nominated for a Pushcart Prize. She is a former lawyer and Fulbright-Nehru Scholar, has an MFA in fiction from the Iowa Writers' Workshop, is working on her second novel and spends a lot of her time in the 13th century. Find out more at shebakarim.com.

ALCHEMY

The Tranquebar Book of Erotic Stories II

Edited by
SHEBA KARIM

TRANQUEBAR PRESS
An imprint of westland ltd

Venkat Towers, 165, P.H. Road, Maduravoyal, Chennai 600 095
No. 38/10 (New No.5), Raghava Nagar, New Timber Yard Layout, Bangalore 560 02
23/181, Anand Nagar, Nehru Road, Santacruz East, Mumbai 400 055
93, Ist Floor, Sham Lal Road, Daryaganj, New Delhi 110 002

First published in India in TRANQUBEAR by westland ltd 2012

10 9 8 7 6 5 4 3 2 1

ISBN: 978-93-82618-03-4

Typeset by FourWords Inc.

Printed at Thomson Press (India) Ltd.

... yeh bata charagar
Teri zambil men
Nuskha-e kimiya-e muhabbat bhi hai?

... tell me, healer
In your wondrous bag
Is there a cure for the alchemy of love?

~ *Ek Chameli Ke Mandve Tale*, Makhdoom Mohiuddin

CONTENTS

Introduction ix

The Farmer's Daughter
Rabi Thapa 1

Clay
Gudiya 16

Sanskrit
Ranbir Sidhu 39

Abandon
Shrimoyee Nandini 59

Mouth
M. Svairini 72

A Foreigner
Amitava Kumar 104

SEMEN, SALIVA, SWEAT, BLOOD
Hansda Sowvendra Shekhar 119

F IS FOR FIRE
Abeer Hoque 145

THE PERISCOPE
Lopa Ghosh 157

THE MATINEE
Mohan Sikka 171

THE MARRYING KIND
Mary Anne Mohanraj 183

THE MONK
Ananda Devi 197

NEXT YEAR AT THE TAJ
Sheba Karim 215

Contributors 230

Acknowledgments 233

INTRODUCTION

When I agreed to edit this anthology, I believed I had quite the challenge ahead. To put together an anthology of creative, well-crafted stories is, in and of itself, no easy task. To find creative, well-crafted stories in which sex is integral to the narrative is even more difficult; in spite of it being one of our primary motivators and a natural activity essential to both the survival and sanity of the human race, most accomplished writers will tell you it's pretty damn hard to write about sex. Now, further limit the criteria by requiring the stories be written by writers of South Asian descent, and well, you understand my initial trepidation.

But I needn't have worried. I reviewed the submissions for this book on a road trip from New York to New Mexico. As we passed through a long stretch of America's conservative Bible belt, Tennessee, Arkansas, Oklahoma, Texas, where giant billboards remind you that it's still not too late to repent your sins and be saved by Jesus, male preachers call homosexuality an abomination on the radio and Planned Parenthood may soon become as extinct as the dinosaurs, I read and reread stories of fornication and desire. By the time we reached the stark, enchanted landscapes of New Mexico, *Alchemy* had begun to take shape.

For a certain reading public in this country, an erotica anthology is no longer a naughty novelty but has been accepted as a genre capable of literary merit. The first anthology, *Electric Feather: The Tranquebar Book of Erotic Stories*, has been followed by *Blue: The Tranquebar Book of Erotic Stories from Sri Lanka* and *Close, Too Close: The Tranquebar Book of Queer Erotica*, among others. I'm writing this introduction at a time when the morality policing of Mumbai's nightlife is making headlines and cases continue to be filed throughout the country based on the 'hurt sentiments' laws. When the hurt sentiments laws were introduced in the colonial era, 'an underlying assumption was that there was a need for a rational and neutral arbiter (the colonial State) to govern the relationship between "emotionally excitable subjects" prone to emotional injury and physical violence.'[1] Though the British rulers have left, the colonial hangover continues; hurt sentiments laws continue to be one of the country's greatest threats to freedom of speech and artistic expression, allowing a criminal case to be filed against an author (or journalist, or painter, or cartoonist) based on a

[1] Lawrence Liang, 'Love Language or Hate Speech', *Tehelka*, Volume 9, Issue 9, March 3, 2012.

completely subjective claim of 'hurt feelings' rather than, for example, an actual incitement toward violence. In an environment where antiquated laws are used to harass, threaten and control, the Health minister says sex between men is completely unnatural and should not happen while speaking at an HIV/AIDS conference, rape victims are told they were 'asking for it' and there is a movement to reinstate Section 377, erotica anthologies continue to be brave books, which, in their own ways, help push back against forces which would prefer to silence the discourse on sexual freedom rather than engage in it.

Just as alchemists have tried to combine various base metals and substances in an attempt to transmute them into gold, and, in so doing, discover the elixir of life, so many elements of ourselves come together in the act of sex: skin and bodily fluids, desire, fear, greed, joy, stigma, pride, affection, guilt, often in the hope of creating something more beautiful, our personal elixirs of life, however temporary, however permanent. The stories in the anthology address our own attempts at alchemy. Some might make you hot. Some might make you laugh, or wince, or wonder. One or two might even break your heart.

However it touches you (or makes you want to be touched), it is my sincere hope that you enjoy reading this anthology as much as I have enjoyed editing it.

SHEBA KARIM
Siolim, Goa
July 2012

THE FARMER'S DAUGHTER

Rabi Thapa

I ONCE READ A STORY about a college boy who fancies his maid, an onanistic indulgence, indeed one that had been declared as such by reviewers so young that even in this new age of discos and cabin restaurants and bike rides with beaus, they would not have had the chance to get fucked. The story was clearly a fantasy, but it was amusing to hear the oldies croaking about misrepresentation and the kiddies citing Freud, both saying No Sex Please, We're Nepalese.

But it must happen, right? Love across the lines. We all know the aristocrats of old regularly alchemized rosy-cheeked scullions into snooty concubines. Half the blue bloods in this country must be bastards and anyway, truth is stranger than fiction.

So here she is, the farmer's daughter, perched on the bed, my bed, combing out her hair, her long, black hair, as I loll casually on the sofa across the room, pretending to read the papers. Ex-Minister Absconds With Secretary, Sexual Mores Declining, Street Walkers On The Run and I might add, What The Fuck Is Going On?

Simply put, nothing is going on. Or something is going on, but while it's undeniably diverting to nudge it along, nothing of import will actually happen. What could happen between a forty-something divorced development consultant (with a specialization in gender) and a farmer's twenty-something married daughter (with a specialization in gendered tasks)?

Sumati Maharjan is my maid. She's beautiful, a real fox if such a term can be applied to a young woman seemingly without guile, and weighed down by the reality of her day to day life. The hours she spends at mine twice a week—washing and mopping and dusting—qualify as blessed respite from the drudgery of working the family's diminishing squares of shit-specked soil for no more reward than the heavy hand of her drunken husband. Who must suffer from a local variant of brewer's droop that makes him shrink from the comforts of Sumati's generous curves, for surely she would not feel easy on another man's bed if she were committed to her own.

Yes, she's told me her life story. And what a cliché of a sob story it is in this country of abused wives, sisters, daughters: the junior bride in a broken joint family, with not even the support of her *maiti* (having lost her parents early on), living only for her five-year-old son.

'What does your husband do?'

'He drinks.'

What has it to do with me? I can't pretend that I am especially concerned about her wellbeing, these tragic tales are a dime a dozen in this benighted country and god knows I've interviewed my share of oppressed women. But I'm interested enough to draw her out; perhaps she's more of a personal project than those I discuss in the five-star seminar rooms of the capital. It has nothing to do with me, unless I choose to touch her. That isn't going to happen right now, and not just because of the abyss of ten feet between us. For the moment it's not even, what did I call it, an onanistic indulgence. She's on my bed not because she's inviting me to join her, but because I invited her in from the kitchen, it's payday. There's nowhere else to sit in my overpriced studio but on the sofa next to me, and that wouldn't quite do.

She's finished for the day, and has showered in my bathroom before she heads back across the temple square to her crowded quarters. Even this is less familiarity than convenience—a solar-charged shower being vastly preferable to a cold bucket wash—but the thought of her naked behind a flimsy ply of wood is more excitement than I'm used to. So she combs out her long, black hair in deliberate, sweeping movements, and I watch her over the top of the paper, wondering what it would be like to grab a handful and pull on it.

'What are you looking at?'

'... Hm?'

'Why are you looking?'

'I'm thinking of my own hair when I was a student. I used to hate combing it out, but you seem to enjoy it.'

'You had long hair?'

'Sure did. I was a *hero*.'

'You're not a hero anymore?'

'Now I'm old, what hero.'

Sumati smiles and resumes those long, silky movements. But she stops too soon, ties her still-damp hair into a knot, and looks at me expectantly.

'What happened?'

'Um, if you're going to pay me today, could you give me something for Dasain as well? We have a lot of festival expenses—'

'Oh ... a Dasain bonus? What are you going to buy?'

'Well, I need to buy some clothes for my son ...'

'Hm. And for yourself? Will your husband buy you a sari or something?'

'That man?' She laughs, but without bitterness. She seems to find the idea of her alcoholic, unemployed husband doing anything to please her genuinely amusing. Why would he, when he could spend the equivalent on a few jugs of local raksi.

I don't question her home economics any further. 'Okay then. Take.'

She approaches, and I try the cheap trick of holding on to the notes a moment too long. She lets go and regards me quizzically. I quickly offer the money to her again and say, almost as an afterthought, 'Buy something for yourself as well.'

She turns in the doorway, and I thank god that even the dowdiest maxi coat, when framed against sunshine, is made over into a poor man's Arabian Nights fantasy. I can discern the shape of her body from the underside of her breasts to her hips, her thighs down to her calves, and I want to explore this newly revealed landscape.

'For myself?'

'Yes, buy a kurta or something. You should think of your own happiness sometimes.'

I'm forced to reconsider the propriety of the friendly terms I've established with Sumati, that's to say Look Don't Touch, when she turns up on a windblown, cold day wearing a brand spanking new kurta, and gets down on her knees to mop the floor. The absurdity of the tableau is rather eased by how desirable she looks in this figure-hugging outfit, sequins and all, but it's absurd nonetheless. I can't keep my eyes off her, and I'm positive I'm going to miss the day's deadline for handing in a report on gender violence in South Asia. Threading my way through statistics on rape and incest and the whole range of sexual violence our repressed men visit upon our women, I want to violate Sumati. She is terribly distracting today, and the usual peeks over the top of my laptop do not suffice.

In her new kurta, she is transformed from a pretty drudge into a sexy, modern Nepali woman, a world away from the farmer's daughter I can't possibly mess around with because of this, that and the other. Her allure is magnified by the fact that she not only bought a kurta with the money I gave her, she *put it on for me*, festival or no. I see her slipping on the starched kurta in front of a cracked mirror, straining to make out how she looks in a badly lit room, and lying to her family as she leaves her place for mine. It's unaccountably bold on her part, and the development feels dangerous. Unable to consider the implications with her bustling about, I head out for coffee. Away from the flat, I can almost forget that Sumati is in it.

When I get back, she asks if I would like a cup of tea—the first time she's done that—and though I'd like to grab her by the waist and pull her towards me, I nod and sink into the sofa. It occurs to me again that, in a kurta, she could be one of my uppity female colleagues, salving her conscience by working for her downtrodden counterparts. I've often daydreamed about sweeping one of these ladies off her feet and onto a conference table, here's to filling in the gender gap, thank you ma'am. But I can't quite picture myself kissing my maid.

Sumati's now at the threshold of the room, with two mugs of tea. She hasn't bothered to fish out a humble steel cup for herself, as one might expect, we are both drinking from matching ceramic cups in elegant pastel. Should I invite her to sit with me on the sofa? Master and maid sharing a cup of tea on the sofa, how cute, how enlightened, *quel scandale!* I'd laugh if my armpits weren't damp with sudden sweat. She approaches, all innocence.

I don't invite her to sit next to me. I take the cup of tea, and admire her smooth brown back as she turns to go. '... Ey, your kurta's zip isn't done properly,' I exclaim.

She looks embarrassed. *'Ho ra?'*

'Yes,' I grin. 'Shall I do it up? I guess you can't reach.' I place my cup of tea on the arm of the sofa, but stay put. 'Why don't you sit down, how can I reach from here,' I say in a businesslike tone. She obeys, sitting at an angle. But the sofa's luxurious give has her listing towards me, and she leans away in compensation.

I find myself staring at her bare back. The zip has come undone to just above the bra line, the flaps of gauzy mauve like giant petals. I want to touch her skin, brushing along the faint line of down tracing her spine. My fingers move to restore normality. But they manage to get themselves tangled up, and slip from zip to skin, cold digits probing her warm body. '*Achooo!*' she protests. 'Don't move!' I command. 'This is a bit tight. Can you bring your shoulders back a bit, a bit straight?' She obliges, pushing her bosom out tantalisingly, the skin below my fingers creasing deliciously. *Zipppp!* 'There,' I say, tapping her redundantly on the shoulder. 'Done.' She holds still a moment longer, and I mutter, 'Very nice kurta this is. Looks good on you.' She drawls out an exaggerated, 'Thyaank yoo', and I wish I'd unzipped her instead. But she is on her feet already, and now she sits on my bed with her cup of tea and we consider each other like freshly-surfaced sea creatures, with curious wariness. My eyes drop down to my lap, and I notice my arousal. I reach for a book. She drinks her tea, blank-faced, looking out the window into the slanting rays of the evening sun. Then she leaves, and I close my eyes and conjure up her warm skin, the way it moved under my fingers.

The next day, I think about how close we came to ... what? Even if I interpreted her wearing of the kurta favourably, would she really have allowed me to divest her of it? Ironically, were I to dispossess her of that signification of modernity, that which intensified my attraction to her, it would be clear how similar we all are at skin level. We all aspire to live a little better—to enjoy that hot shower, to wear that new kurta, to drink tea in pastel shades—how much did it matter that we moved in wholly different worlds?

Too often, I'd leered at buxom village women bathing under the community taps or parried the suggestive remarks of the charming ladies running lodges along hiking trails while other men, comfortable with taking what they could get, ended the richer for it. I worked to uplift oppressed women, but I couldn't think of fucking one of them—would the act constitute upliftment or exploitation? I convince myself that no one need be the wiser for the solace Sumati and I might find in one another.

The days stall in a buzz of anticipation. I feel maybe it is all in my mind, that the familiar sight of Sumati's faded maxis will extinguish my infatuation. But I clear away meetings on the Saturday she is next due, and plot multiple narratives that all end with her naked in my bed. Should I wait for her to finish work, and call her in for a cup of tea? Or should I approach her when she is least expecting it? I recall the more modern modes of seduction I picked up in movies and applied with variable success in my younger days in *pharen*, before I flirted with a Nepali marriage and its parched aftermath. Via glass of wine, moonlit walk or neon club, I'd essayed moves that invariably led to a politely suggestive *I feel like kissing you* ... I can't imagine anything more risible than trying to seduce Sumati while she is washing my dirty clothes, or mopping the floor. I visualise myself creeping up while she is doing the dishes and cupping her breasts from behind, kissing her damp neck, leaning into her buttocks. But the fog of my sensuous imaginings is rent by her shrieks, and I see my awkward moves stutter into humiliation. The days of flinging stable maids onto piles of hay are over in Kathmandu, yet we can't drink anything stronger than tea together. I decide to trust to instinct.

On the morning of the Saturday I am expecting Sumati, I spot her in the neighbourhood market. She is wearing her new kurta, and is accompanied by a shrunken, dark gnome of a man. The way she meekly follows him as he pushes through the crowds tells me that he is her husband. I retreat to the pavement and watch them approach. Sumati looks as desirable as ever, but her link to this man debases her to his scruffy, puff-eyed level. I realise that the dismissiveness with which she talks about him is mere bravado. She is bound to him by an invisible thread, and walks with her face turned to the ground. As they pass his eyes scan the pavement and stop on mine.

My heart lurches. Then I remember he doesn't even know I exist. Sumati has told her family she is working for a married couple because, she claims, they wouldn't approve of a single man (divorced, to boot). But the meanness of her husband's expression leaves me in no doubt as to whom it is she doesn't want to upset. He's short and scrawny, but I can guess what he and his brothers might be capable of if they get a sniff of what I am planning this afternoon.

I shudder, and as they merge into the chaotic architecture of the old city I promise not to interfere with the man's god-given rights over Sumati. I chastise myself for ever believing my interest in her was more than a sordid fantasy, and one with potentially catastrophic consequences. What I'd disingenuously posited as a 'social experiment' would in all likelihood have been construed by Sumati as an alternative—for herself and her son—to the life that had been written for her with her repulsive husband, and where would I be then? I quickly make plans to spend the day in the city.

Najane gaon ko bato nasodhnu, they say. Don't ask the way to a village you're not going to visit. So I avoid Sumati, keeping to myself when she's around. I realize she must be puzzled, even hurt by my coldness, but every time I catch myself looking at her, the pockmarked face of her husband comes between us. It's all for the best, I tell myself, I'm doing us all a favour. The distractions of the festive season do their part.

In the days following Dasain, Sumati comes up to me and my sofa, looking like the jilted lover that never was. She stands over me, and I am compelled to face her sulky features. But she says nothing, and I feel bad.

'What happened?'

She remains silent, and I know we can't really talk about what she wants to talk about.

'Work done?'

She nods.

'Then ...' I begin to fidget.

'It's been over a month ...'

A month since? It occurs to me that I haven't paid her, so keen have I been on staying out of her way. 'Oh, wait,' I mutter with relief. I reach for my wallet and count out the notes. She takes them, and makes as if to leave.

'I saw you in the market during Dasain,' I blurt out.

'*Ho?*'

'Yes, with your husband, you were ... wearing your new kurta. It was a Saturday.'

'Who are you talking about?'

'Your husband ... that dark guy walking with you?'

Her puzzled expression changes to one of scornful amusement. 'You thought that old guy was my husband? That's my oldest brother-in-law! How could I marry someone who looked like that! *Chyaa!*' She titters, raising a hand to cover her mouth, and I remember that hers was a love marriage, after all. I see a strong young man, his looks marred by the genie in the bottle, with a sensitive cast of features. Someone more like what I used to be, but whose wife hadn't had the sense to excise him before it was too late. I really need to do all of us a favour, I conclude, as Sumati folds the bills into her bosom, giggling.

The old familiarity blooms between us again, courtesy of our now customary cups of tea, and we chat at length. She answers my questions about her farming community and their changing place in the urban milieu hemming them in. I answer her questions about the world outside the triangle of farm, home and market. In between, we venture into the interstices of our lives, where few others care to tread. Why did I get divorced? Does she ever think of getting divorced? What was my wife like? What is her husband like? Why did I never have children? Will she have more children? What do I want? What does she want?

Late one morning, I am watching Sumati sweep the terrace, bent double. She has taken to wearing kurtas regularly, plain numbers she probably reserved for trips to the market before she decided to wear them for me. It's a warm day, and even from inside, I can make out the dark patches of sweat under her arms. I move closer to the window, leaning against it with a book in hand. She is fifteen feet away, facing me, and the surprisingly low-cut kurta reveals more than I'd hoped for. The movements of her arms alternately shield and reveal her breasts, jostling them together within the cups of her workaday brassiere. Even with the wire gauze of the window between us, I fancy I can see her tan cleavage glistening. My breath stops. Then she turns, offering me a brief profile before the baggy kurta obscures all. I wait. When she turns around again, I'm ready. Those luscious half-moons float in the faded fabric, straining against the buttons, and I'm in heaven.

She looks up suddenly, forehead creased, and meets my gaze. I drop my eyes to the book immediately, frozen in my stance. A few seconds pass, and I brace myself, expecting her to say something. Then the scrape of the broom resumes, more slowly. I look up, then stare openly. Two of the three buttons are now undone. The blood rushes. I gape at her breasts, swaying gently, occasionally a glimpse of her soft stomach. I can't believe it, she is smiling, sweeping the floor but there is nothing to sweep, and I follow her motions with my own free hand, it doesn't take long at all.

Later, over a solitary dinner, hindsight chides me. *That was it, you fool, you could have had her*. Had I deferred just long enough, long enough to call her in.... She'd stand at the door, feigning a wanton innocence, her kurta unbuttoned, face flushed. I'd tell her to *come here*, why don't you sweep here, sweep the ground beneath my feet. *Where*, she would say, pretending not to understand. *Here*, I would reply, pointing to the floor beneath the sofa on which I sit. *Use a cloth*. She'd return with a wet rag, and get down on her knees in front of me. She would work, and I would watch.

It's Friday night, soon after. I'm out drinking with a British colleague and two of his visiting friends. For their sake, we try not to talk shop but they insist on getting to know the terrain. For the umpteenth time, I trace the constellation of factors that condemns this country to be as associated with material poverty as it is with spiritual wealth. One of the two ladies seems impressed by my knowledge of women's matters, more so as she's inclined to see in every man the chauvinist propping up the patriarchal edifice. I'm impressed by her snub-nosed freckledom, and her heavy, sensual body in smart trekking pants and tee, not bad for forty.

It's not my style, really, but then I wouldn't have thought to pleasure myself in the presence of the maid, either. So when my colleague starts to grumble about early morning meetings, I ask the ladies if they'd like a nightcap, and thank my stars (or rather the forthrightness of older women who know what they want) when after a brief discussion Snubnose decides to accompany me alone to my flat and a bottle of whisky. My colleague is shocked, I can see, but I'm burning.

Back at mine, the moon eyeing us coolly from behind a light veil, Snubnose tucks into the whisky. Soon we move from sofa to bed, from kiss to grope. I turn the lights off, she protests, but I tell her the moonlight will be plenty. As we tussle in the silver shadows, her features are softened into strangeness, and she is and she is not Snubnose. I fling the bedclothes off and strip her to her lacy underwear, then begin tonguing her roughly, thinking, would Sumati let me do this to her? Snubnose moans gratifyingly, and the question flashes across my mind, *how do poor people have sex?* I move up her pale belly and greedily take her hard, pink nipples into my mouth, one by one. They feel like berries between my lips. She moans some more and I straddle her, knees pushing into her armpits, and thrust my penis into her deep cleavage. I close my eyes, and see Sumati's unbuttoned kurta inviting me, her firm, dark-nippled breasts enveloping me. Snubnose giggles incongruously, perhaps she cannot believe that I would make so bold, so I move up and stop her mouth. She does what I want her to do, and I can't help it, I am done, undone. We drift off into a drunken slumber.

But I said older women know what they want, and I have no complaints when I awake to a hand on my crotch. Snubnose rouses me in her mouth, she's still hungry from the night before and knows where to start because this is no sensual, libatory moonlit night, it's bright light streaming in through the windows, and this time I need her to be my farmer's daughter, not the older woman not of my dreams. I let her suck me, smiling at how I'd have to coax Sumati into doing this to me, and when she stalls, looking up to whisper 'Fuck me, fuck me *now*', I flip her around and plunge into her, hard, pulling on her hair while she clutches the sheets. I'm not going to last long, but that's fine because Snubnose is already going 'yes yes yes' like she's never had it so good, and I'm melting molten inside her thinking *I'm fucking Sumati I'm going to fuck Sumati I'm going to fuck Sumati today* when a shadow falls across the bed and I look up to see Sumati standing at the window looking in while I'm comically coming and she's staring at me and Snubnose's face in the pillow yelping 'don't stop don't stop' and I'm molten and frozen and I have never seen such an expression as the one on her face as she turns, turns, and walks away.

CLAY

Gudiya

It was only when Vidu pulled away abruptly and rushed towards the window that Niharika realized that it had stood open all the while.

Vidu's bedroom was on the ground floor and the lawn outside stretched out a hard green. In the time it took for Vidu to pull the shutters and return to bed, Niharika's mind had padded across juicy neon clumps of grass, to a pair of lean chocolate legs squatting near the sweet williams.

What was the gardener's name, she wondered as she shrugged off her bra. And what was he thinking if he had been watching her all this while—bare-bottomed, with the young master between her legs? Perhaps he had been watching. He had looked at her very directly when he opened the gate earlier in the afternoon.

She had had to wait today since the watchman had taken the day off. The gardener was supposed to double up on gate duty—keeping an ear cocked for the bell, rushing to open the gate for visitors who arrived in cars, making careful judgments about who might be close enough to the family to park within the bungalow's premises and who might be an upstart executive who must be told quite firmly that parking inside was impossible.

After she had honked long and impatiently, the gardener finally appeared. Even so, he didn't rush; he strolled up to the gate and the way he looked at her, Niharika felt as if he knew what she was here for.

Until then, she had not spoken to him or even looked at him closely. She only saw him twenty feet off. He was often lingering in the background, beside neat rows of pansies and snapdragons, or fussing over an eccentric pine tree that was reduced to weeping like a willow in this miserable Delhi summer.

Today, as he stood peering into the open car window, she looked at the gardener. He was wearing one of those loose striped undershorts that seem to be the uniform of the toiling male masses around here. His chest was bare, smooth, the fragrance of wet, thirsty June earth coming off his frame. It was as if he was carved from a slab of pure dark chocolate, or an idol made out of the buttery clay from the Yamuna, one that had never quite dried or hardened.

Niharika wondered where he was from. With those emphatic bones and easy gait, he could well be from the traditional maali caste. Or he could be a tribal from somewhere in the central belt. It was a face and body straight out of the tourism board's promotional posters—quiet but not hostile, lean without being hungry. No heavy-duty muscles. Just a body that seemed content to be what it was—strong, unhurried and unashamed.

But from her new lover Vidu, it was pointless expecting unselfconsciousness. He never even bothered to take off his t-shirt, nor did he ask her to take off hers. The first couple of times, he had kissed her for a minute and then pulled off his jeans.

Maybe Vidu just didn't think of himself as naked as long as he had his shirt on. Maybe he never took all his clothes off for a woman. Or maybe it was just her. Why go slow, why stroke and strip and slide a tongue across earlobes and nipples when he knew he could leap across to a straight fuck?

Probably that. Vidu wasn't about to give her anything he didn't have to. He didn't give much of himself that way. There was little conversation, hardly any hugging or kissing. She even suspected that if his undies weren't so tight he wouldn't have bothered to take those off either. Even so, there were small comforts. At least, Vidu wasn't a boxer boy.

If there was one thing she'd learnt to take seriously over the years, it was small comforts. A clean room, a well-made Bloody Mary, stiff canvas napkins folded properly, soft toilet paper, interesting tiles. Small things made the man. And in her experience, men who wore checked boxers under boot cut Levis were emotionally and sexually lazy. She particularly couldn't stand the carefully scruffy, foreign-return boys who usually wore said boxers and t-shirts with some vaguely political slogan.

On the other hand, snug white or black v-front undies often spelt out 'narcissist'. Full of pretend machismo.

Niharika had decided they were too busy just existing for public benefit to be of much personal use. She preferred Vidu's type. Tight brown underpants that covered an inch of thigh. Not unlike the shorts that some girls wore to the Vasant Vihar market these days, usually leggy girls from the international schools. Niharika felt intensely grateful she was too old to compete with their Barbie limbs.

But seeing a similar pair of shorts on Vidu was nice. She could see the shape of his power yoga buttocks. It meant he wanted to be looked at, wanted to be wanted. That was one good thing. And there were his good teeth, his struggling actor's body.

Part-actor, part-singer, part-philosopher—that's how he'd been introduced at Rizo's party. Poor Rizo. He'd taken some pains—gold class tickets at the movie, the wining-dining shosha. But what to do? Rizo was just not her type. He turned out to be a good sport anyway. When he caught her checking out Vidu, he introduced them at once. Perhaps he was generous. Or maybe he was just sick of her no-touching act and thought it would be fun to see what his pal could get out of the ice-box. Men were strange that way.

She was certain Rizo had heard about her and Vidu and these afternoon sessions. Discretion wasn't a strong point with Delhi boys. But Niharika was past caring. She was determined to make the most of a reasonably hunky guy who could quote Goethe, wore tight brown undies, and took his manhood seriously enough to work hard on his body.

True, her joy in Vidu dimmed when she saw the way he used his Goethe-reading voice to place himself at the centre of attention at every party. She had been annoyed at the way he used the word 'soul' three times within ten minutes of being introduced. The way his eyes constantly darted around the room—who just walked in, who might be useful. At Rizo's party, all the women had scrutinized him, and by extension, her, wondering, no doubt, what the plump chick with the cheap bag had done to deserve the stud.

He had talked exclusively to her for an hour when a large woman in blingy chiffon beckoned with a half-wave. He'd gone over at once, whispering: 'It's work, sweets! You know I have to deal with work wherever I go, yeah?'

Niharika resented that he was treating her like a jealous girlfriend. She resented the apologetic way he ran the tip of his tongue across his sharp little front teeth and let his eyes dance, as if silently laughing at her jealousy. Yet, she decided to sleep with him.

He was in town for only a few weeks. If the fates were offering a tall, good-looking young man, why resist? Life was made up of small incentives.

When the blingy cow was done sparkling at him, Vidu had returned to Niharika's side and offered to drop her home. She'd said, 'No thanks. I have a car.' And before he could mention safety etcetera, she added, 'And I'm the best drunk driver I know.'

She did exchange phone numbers though, and she did answer the text message he sent at three in the morning. And she did promise to join him for lunch at his place.

Over the phone, he'd promised to show her the family heirlooms, daguerreotypes and etchings. It had made Niharika bubble with laughter. Daguerreotypes! Who used such excuses these days? 'Dinner' or even just 'coffee' was euphemism enough. 'Daguerreotypes' was overkill. But now that she'd seen the 'family home', she understood why he brought it up.

It was a colonial bungalow with more rooms than they knew what to do with, surrounded on three sides by sweet-smelling grass, flowers and an obviously suffering pine tree. These people probably had more daguerreotypes than she had plastic hair clips.

Later, Niharika tried teasing him. 'Weren't you going to show me your family heirlooms?' she had said, to which a man of quicker wit might have responded by saying, 'I did. But you had your eyes closed all the time.'

But Vidu didn't have the presence of mind. He just smiled slyly, as if the little deception of heirlooms was something other than a joke. In any case, playful banter was not on his agenda. Nor hers. Banter and laughter was the stuff of attachment, which she could ill-afford. He was only here for a few weeks, after all, and she was determined to make the most of it, and then retreat with minimum damage to her heart.

But on her first visit, she was unnerved when she discovered that they weren't alone in the house. An elder brother was upstairs, in the library. Vidu's father was at work but his mother was out shopping and might return any minute. His grandmother was taking a nap in a 'sun room' and a toddler called Fish wandered in and out of rooms, moving her head to some internal, inaudible music.

Vidu, being generally jobless, was supposed to watch Fish until one of the other adults showed up. But his idea of babysitting was limited to craning his neck every fifteen minutes to check whether the kid was still alive, and if she was, to give her a lazy wink and a flying kiss.

Niharika was introduced with a 'Say hello to aunty', but before the poor mite had a chance to take all four fingers out of her mouth and show off her good manners, Vidu had ushered Niharika into his bedroom.

She had only had a second to turn around and call out 'Hello, little girl' before the bedroom door slammed shut.

She had been nervous—the old-world opulence, the hard bright sun, the utter silence, a grandmother snoring in the next room, a toddler at the door. But Vidu had given her the full benefit of his even teeth.

She had returned his smile and some of the awkwardness melted. In less than thirty seconds, she was on her back and he was yanking shafts of denim down her calves, sliding the fabric over her heels. He didn't bother with the blouse, of course. He didn't wait for her to roll down her panties before cupping her pubis with his hand. A minute later, he was sliding his fingers out of her. He rubbed the tip of his penis against the rim of her vagina. She parted easily for him and held him firm inside. Then he was moving. Seconds later, the hammering began.

Fish was calling out 'Unca-unca-unca-unca' with scarcely a stop for breath and beating her fists on the door.

Niharika was glad. Now there was a real dash of urgency to the proceedings, which had been too practised for her liking so far. It was almost as if Vidu did the same thing every day and knew exactly how to whisk off the woman of the day to his bed in thirty seconds flat, and off with the panties please.

The child's sweet, frantic voice and Vidu's panicked eyes told her that the expected pattern had been broken. She was glad. Vidu paused for just a second and then his hips began to move faster. 'Answer,' Niharika had urged him even as she started to move her hips under his. But he was silent. The knocking went on.

Niharika had bitten his shoulder and said, 'If she starts crying she'll bring the house down. She'll wake up your grandmother. Answer!'

So Vidu had to break rhythm as he raised his head and shouted, 'Yes, sweetie pie. Five minutes. Uncle is in the bathroom.'

Niharika had giggled although Vidu clearly didn't think it was funny. Still, the giggle was well-timed. It restored Vidu's smile and he went back to work at a frantic pace. She had smiled too. He seemed to want to work hard and power yoga was clearly a good thing. He came a few minutes later, after she did, and he pulled out in time. There was no time for cuddles or coital musing, of course, but that was probably for the best.

And so, that first afternoon, Niharika had decided it wasn't bad having Fish around. The interruption had thrown Vidu off track. He dropped the practised mannerisms and the real, boyish creature showed through.

Besides, the kid was cute. As soon as they unlocked the door, Fish had announced that she was hungry. But she wasn't hungry for the lunch the cook had already prepared. She was hungry for 'pakkek unca-style'.

So Vidu had stepped into the kitchen to fix pancakes, Vidu-style. He didn't seem to mind and, after a moment's hesitation, he'd asked Niharika to join them in the kitchen. She had ended up with Fish in her lap, forking small squares of fat pancakes doused in Amul butter and Dabur honey, carefully putting them in the toddler's waiting mouth.

Niharika didn't like to get involved with families. But here she was, in the kitchen with a lisping child in her lap. Vidu's sweat was still drying on her breasts, and with all those familiar household sights and smells—butter in its translucent white and blue wrapping, the hefty glass bottle of Dabur honey, the sticky spoons and knives—it was impossible not to feel at home.

Perhaps some of that warm familiarity had rubbed off on Vidu. He smiled contently across the table and asked if she would like to come back for lunch tomorrow. Instead of answering him directly, Niharika found herself putting her lips against the toddler's curly head.

'What does Fish think? Should aunty come again tomorrow?'

She did return the next day and she was, and wasn't disappointed in the same ways. Again, Vidu worked hard at making her come before he did. Again, no fondling or cuddling. Nobody else joined them for lunch—it was just her, Vidu and Fish. The cook quietly entered the kitchen at two in the afternoon and took a tray up to Fish's dad, who was busy researching something. Their grandmother snored in the sun room. Apparently, the old lady was never woken up. When she called out in a tremulous, angry voice, the cook would take a tray with either breakfast or dinner, depending on how low the sun hung in the sky. The only other sign of life around the place was the smooth brown figure hunched over the fragrant lawn. He was trimming the grass that day and the strong, green smell hung in the air like summer's promise.

Niharika wondered about the parents. Did they know Vidu was bringing women over in the afternoon? Didn't the elder brother worry about Fish, and what she might be exposed to? Poor Fish. She must wonder why uncle and aunty both had to use the bathroom together. Perhaps she thought one of them wasn't properly potty-trained.

But she was not supposed to think of Vidu's family. Vidu was only here for another two weeks. She needed to focus on what she could hope to get. How many times could she hope to be invited over? She always waited for Vidu to renew the invitation. 'What are you doing the day after?' 'Do you want pizza tomorrow?'

It would always be hurried, of course. Vidu wasn't going to make it slow and tender, she knew. But that was alright. It was good. She didn't want tenderness. She wanted orgasms. She had had two already. And if he asked her over even on alternate days, she would get more. Four, five, six?

She had to give him that. Vidu wasn't selfish or unthinking in bed. He would keep going if she whispered 'keep going'. 'It is more than good,' she told herself. 'Five or six orgasms is more than what some women get in a lifetime. Fuck slow and tender. Just keep showing up.'

And show up she did. Today was her fourth time here. Because of the kid standing right outside the door, they had been careful not to make a sound. But it was getting harder to manage Fish.

After lunch—today Fish had insisted that aunty feed her with her own hands—the kid tried to follow them into the bedroom. Vidu had a hard time explaining that uncle and aunty had to talk about something important; they couldn't be disturbed. The poor kid kept promising she would not disturb; she was just going to play with her crayons in a corner.

Her lonely eyes had nearly killed the sexual charge. Niharika couldn't bring herself to shut the door on that baby face. But Vidu was firm. He took Fish into the sun room and set her in a low chair, next to his sleeping grandmother. He put a thick notebook and a set of crayons in front of her and told her to draw for at least fifteen minutes.

There was reason to hurry today. And yet, as Vidu pulled off his jeans and reached for her, Niharika began to unbutton her blouse.

He looked mildly surprised, then quickly jumped off the bed and ran to shut the window. She stretched full-length and wondered why Vidu suddenly felt the need for privacy. The window had stood open the last few times she was here, after all. Did he think it was okay for the gardener to witness the act, but not to look at their bare chests?

It was the first time he was seeing her naked. He touched one bare breast tentatively and was about to slide his fingers down her stomach when she caught his fingers and drew them back upwards. His palm slid up to cup the underside of her right breast. When his thumb pressed the side of the nipple, she reached for his other hand and placed it on the left breast.

A steady throb hung between his legs. He was ready, waiting for a sign from her. She was already wet and wanted him inside her but his hands were stroking her neck and she didn't want him to stop. He lay on top of her and rubbed himself up and down her body. She allowed herself a very soft moan. His hand slid down and began to pry into her crotch. She resisted for a second then parted her legs a few inches. His fingers touched the wetness between her thighs. Quickly Vidu hooked his hands under her knees and pushed her legs apart.

Four minutes ticked past faster than they should have, and Fish was back at the door, calling 'unca-unca-unca'. Vidu's throat tightened with annoyance. He wanted to ignore her but Niharika insisted that he answer. 'She won't go away until you do.'

She shifted her hips so that his penis slipped out of her. Vidu sighed, craned his neck towards the door and shouted, 'Five minutes! Do your crayons, sweetie pie. Uncle is coming.'

Then he pressed his mouth hard on Niharika's before she could say another word. A shiver of pleasure coursed up her belly. And the child's small voice drifted in again, 'But alledy I did cayon. I don want to do more cayon.'

Vidu's eyes met Niharika's. A tiny smile flitted back and forth. He raised his head again and shouted back, 'Do some more. Colour all the pages.'

A second of silence, then the sound of light feet padding away. Niharika took Vidu's lower lip between her teeth and bit. Her hands went down to her own crotch, found the tip of his penis and brushed it lightly against her vagina. She moved her hips until he was an inch further inside. Then Vidu's pelvis was pushing hard against hers.

He began to move faster, his face burrowing into the side of her neck. She turned her face towards the window, and then she saw the shadow. She blinked a few times, squeezed her eyes shut and opened them again. Yes, definitely a shadow. A long column of darkness cutting out two neat shafts of light coming in through the tiny gaps between the shutters.

She gasped slightly. Her hands instinctively went to Vidu's head; she whispered his name and pushed the hair off his forehead. But the gesture seemed to stimulate him. He began to push harder. Niharika gasped again and it seemed like the shadow moved.

It slid downwards until it was barely visible above the windowsill. The green gap where a latch held the shutters down—the green of the grass outside—had suddenly turned brown. Rich, dark brown. Clayey riverbed skin. Or perhaps a brown iris.

What colour were the eyes? Niharika couldn't be certain. Brown? Black? Certainly not grey or green—she'd have remembered that as unusual.

'Vidu,' she whispered again. A muffled 'Yeah' came from the gasping mouth, hot at her neck. His hands were kneading her fleshy buttocks. The shadow at the window was very still. She looked steadily at the tiny gap near the latch. It had not turned green again. Niharika looked away. Her lips brushed Vidu's sweaty forehead.

'Vidu.'

He raised his head slightly this time and stopped moving for a moment. He half-smiled. 'Is something wrong?'

Niharika opened her mouth to say something, but then she didn't. Her hands slid down the back of his neck, moved along his spine. The tips of her fingers traced the crack below. He touched her lips with his. 'Slower,' she said, and turned her face again so that she was facing the window.

Vidu whispered, 'Okay' and his hips began to move again. 'Is that good?'

She lifted her feet so that her knees gripped his flanks. He slipped into a gentle forward-backward rhythm. The shadow moved. The brown eye turned green. Niharika moaned. 'Shh,' warned Vidu.

She stroked his back again. 'Harder now,' she whispered. He grunted softly and obeyed. 'Harder,' she repeated and squeezed the firm muscles of his buttocks.

Her eyes flew open when the knocking began again. A quiet knock at first, but it grew louder with each cry. That small, pleading voice again. 'Unca, o-pin. Gumma call. Unca, o-pin.'

Vidu didn't break his rhythm. Each thrust was rougher than the last and towards the end, Vidu slid his large hands under her hips and raised her pelvis so that she was arching up towards him. The slight shift in position undid the elusive knot of pleasure within her. She gasped as she came. The knocking at the door grew infrequent and then stopped.

Niharika reached for Vidu's head and pulled it down to hers. Her tongue traced the outline of his lips. Vidu looked back into her eyes, confused. They kissed roughly, her teeth on his lips. She was content to just lie back now but a pulse seemed to be throbbing deep inside her. Vidu was still moving, panting hard. She broke the kiss and moved under him, making slow, tiny circles with her hips. Her fingers traced circular patterns on his spine with the sweat running off his skin. Noisy grunts escaped him with each thrust. He didn't care about being quiet any more.

He was fucking her hard now, and each move shuddered up her pelvis. Then suddenly, he slowed and his hips began to move in slow, gentle circles, like her own. The pulse had turned into a wave and her mouth grew parched. In a minute, she came again. Almost at the same time, Vidu pulled out with a cry.

When their breath quieted down, she adjusted the pillows and lay back in silence. Vidu pulled off his drenched shirt and lay beside her, absently running a finger along her thigh. She turned to the window. The gap between the shutters was green and clear.

'We took much more than fifteen minutes,' she said. Vidu nodded but didn't move. Niharika went into the bathroom and turned on the shower. By the time she stepped out, Vidu had fallen asleep.

She put on her clothes and covered him with a sheet. Then she went to the window and threw it open. The pine was swaying mournfully. A breeze had picked up; dry leaves rustled across a flower bed.

Resting her elbows on the windowsill, she leaned further out and ran her fingers through her wet hair. There was a crackling sound to the right. She turned her head and there he was, near the twin frangipani bushes. Bare, but for his thin striped undershorts.

He was picking up fallen leaves and flowers, putting them into a cane basket, and loosening the soil around the tree. Niharika noticed that his skin matched the colour of the loose, dark soil. She tried to recall what types of soils there were—alluvial, sandy, clay, red?

'So much useless stuff taught, and all at the wrong time!' she thought. Nobody would have taught the gardener, of course. He seemed to be the sort of person who just knew these things. But of course, he couldn't have known. He too would have been taught. Which soil meant what, what it was good for, what to put in it at what time of the year. His kind seemed to know more than what middle school social science taught. Why was information about soils taught under 'social' science rather than science? Of course, they were calling it earth science these days. What would he say if she went up to him and told him that he was like an earth science graduate?

His back was turned to her but he must have sensed her eyes on him. He went around to the other side of the frangipani bush so that he faced her, but he didn't look up. He went on picking up the dry and rotting leaves until there was nothing left to clear. Finally, he raised his head and looked directly into her eyes. There was no smile, or nod, or leer. Steady brown eyes. No looking down or away, after a respectful nod. There was no doubt he had seen.

Niharika withdrew into the bedroom and then quickly walked out of the door, barefoot. She peeped into the sun room first but Fish was missing. The grandmother was asleep. A notebook lay on the floor, a single page stained with squiggles in orange and black.

The living room was empty too. There was a sound in the kitchen but that turned out to be the cook. He grinned when he saw her, bobbing his head up and down by way of greeting, then he picked up a covered tray and disappeared up a flight of stairs.

Of course, the servants would have guessed. A slither of resentment and shame went down her throat and she felt like she would start gagging. Had the gardener already told the others? Had he summoned the cook and watchman in a hurry, asking them to join him at the window?

She shook her wet hair. What did it matter? Probably the servants didn't care. The family certainly didn't seem to care. Perhaps they all needed to pretend they didn't see things if they didn't know how to deal with them. The only casualty would be Fish, of course.

But where was Fish? She looked through a screen door that opened out into the garden and spotted the very clean sole of a tiny shoe. She pushed the door open.

Fish was sitting on an upturned cane basket with her small legs extended, hands folded neatly in her lap, staring into the distance.

'Hello, little girl!' Niharika called out softly. She remembered how much she had disliked adults pouncing on her when she was a kid, trying to surprise her constantly. As if life were an endless game where you waited for large unexpected hands to first frighten you, then coddle you. She herself approached children with caution.

Fish turned, unsmiling. The basket she was sitting on covered a heap of dead leaves and flowers.

'What are you doing out here? Did you get bored of the crayons?'

But the child wouldn't answer.

'Is Fish hungry? Should aunty feed you?'

There was something Fish wanted to say. She was biting her lower lip, frowning. Either she had done something naughty or she was scanning her limited vocabulary for words. Something tightened inside Niharika's chest. She folded the baby fists in one of her hands and gently butted the child's head with her own.

'Little Fish? What happened?'

Fish shrugged. Her thumbnails began to scrape the hands that held hers like an oyster shell. There was a fleck of anxiety in her brown eyes. Niharika's heart began to beat fast.

'Did someone say something? Did Fish see something?'

Niharika butted her head against the child's once more. There was no answer, but Fish leaned forward and butted her head back. It was sign enough. Niharika put her arms around Fish, lifted her off the basket and carried her back into the house. She paused for a moment in the kitchen, wondering what to do. 'Where do you want to sit? At the table?'

A shake of the head.

'Then in the big room? Should we sit on the carpet?' Another shake of the head.

'Then?'

Fish pointed towards the sun room, and Niharika carried her there and tried to set her down on the low chair. But the child's arms clung fiercely to her neck.

'You want to stay in aunty's lap?' Niharika whispered. Silence. Neither a 'yes' nor a 'no', but the warm face was burrowing into the side of her neck.

The grandmother was still asleep in her armchair, feet on the stool. From when she'd first seen the old lady, nothing seemed to have changed except the colour of her sari, and the fact that she had stopped snoring.

Niharika settled into an armchair. Fish was attached to her torso like a baby monkey. She took off the child's shoes, hugged her close. She picked up the notebook and crayons, closed her own hand around the child's and began to draw on a fresh page. The outlines of a room; shafts of sunlight streaming in; a rocking chair; a wrinkled face in profile.

Fish's hand grew resistant. 'Gumma calling unca,' she said.

'Shh!' Niharika whispered. 'Gumma is sleeping. Uncle is also sleeping. We'll make a drawing of her, and then when she wakes up, you can show it to her. Okay?' But the child shook her head firmly. After a pause, she looked up worriedly and pointed to the old lady. 'Gumma sleeping?'

For the first time Niharika looked closely at the shrivelled figure across the room. Strong sunlight beat down from the tall windows, so it was hard to see the features clearly. But even from a distance, she could see that the chest was very still. On a side table, the food tray lay untouched.

Niharika squinted against the light, concentrating on the old woman's profile. She could see now that the mouth was slack; perhaps the eyes were open.

Niharika leaned back in her chair and began to stroke the curls resting on her shoulder. Then she kissed the tip of the child's nose. 'Do you want to go outside? We can play catch on the lawn.'

Fish tilted her head, still staring at Gumma. Then she nodded.

Outside, the sun was still bright. A light breeze sent an odd shiver up her arms. 'It must be past four,' Niharika thought as she settled down on a patch of lawn under the long-suffering pine tree. She reached up and tore off one clump of needles and began to tickle Fish's bare feet.

When the child squealed and rolled away, she chased her all around the tree on her hands and knees, and when she caught up, she grabbed Fish and rolled over and over, her hands laced around the child's head so she wouldn't get hurt. Both of them were laughing when they stopped rolling. The grass made for a soft bed, and it was tall enough to tilt in the direction of the wind. They were content to lie on their backs and squint through the depressing pine branches at shimmering ribbons of sun.

Niharika shut her eyes and began to hum a forgotten ghazal, something about the earth bathing in a drizzle of sunlight. The sun had shifted so that it was directly on her face. She sat up and found that Fish had fallen asleep. Her face felt like toast and she remembered that it wasn't good for children to be out in the summer sun. Her own grandmother had always sent her outdoors with her head covered with a hanky that had been dipped in iced water.

She didn't have a hanky but she did have a dupatta. Niharika stood up and went looking for water. In a corner, she spotted a hosepipe. She walked along the pipe's length until she found the tap, fitted into a wall that was part of a room. There was a clothesline outside with a torn vest, a pair of pants and striped undershorts drying on it.

He's just finished washing up, she guessed. A pool of water stood gleaming under the tap. Was there a bathroom inside the gardener's hut? It didn't look big enough. It was probably a single room with a roll of bedding, a steel trunk, a toilet perhaps. He must bathe and wash clothes in the open air.

Niharika pulled the dupatta off her neck and held it under the tap. The water was warm and it soothed her as only water can. As she bent forward, her flushed face was reflected in the pool at her feet. Against the harsh light and yellow-blue sky, her face looked almost as dark as the mud.

As she walked back to the garden, she ran her fingers along the scratched concrete of the hut. Just before the wall sharpened into a corner, she noticed a window. It stood wide open.

She reminded herself of that detail afterwards—that the window had stood open. She had not come looking for a crack to which she could put her eye. All she did was pause and glance in, by accident almost. He was lying on the floor on a mattress, knees bent, one arm thrown over his face. A clean pair of striped undershorts lay near his feet. His other hand was placed low on his belly.

Niharika stood there, not daring to squint or come any closer. His body seemed dull, as if the brown shine of sun and sweat had been patted down with a light towel and what was left on his skin was a matte lethargy. If she could see his eyes, perhaps they would be dull, rendered black in the fading light.

He stretched his legs and his hand slipped lower, between his legs. Even in the lightless room, she could see that his penis was hard, upright. He was not stroking it or touching it, not yet. A kind of muffled cry seemed to well up in his throat and then he took his arm off his face and began to run both his hands up and down his leathery chest.

She thought his eyes were closed yet, and she quickly ducked and ran back as quietly as she could. Back at the pine tree, she covered Fish's head with the wet dupatta. It would dry off in a few minutes but the sun would have gone down by then.

Niharika shut her eyes. She tried to hum the ghazal but the words now seemed fractured and inelegant. She lay down on the grass and threw both arms over her face, letting the sun darken the underside of her arms. Minutes passed. The sun was suddenly cut out and she didn't need to open her eyes to know that a shadow stood over her.

A spray of water hit her neck. She removed her arms from her face, blinking. Vidu stood there, holding the hosepipe, his thumb blocking off the water temporarily. He looked like he was about ready to drench her thoroughly. She quickly put a finger to her lips and tilted her chin towards Fish.

He tossed the pipe aside, knelt and lifted the sleeping child in his arms. They went back to the house, she following a few steps behind. Why had she been so surprised that it was Vidu standing over her as she lay in the lawn? Who did she expect?

Vidu was saying, 'I'd better take Fish to her room.' Niharika nodded and glanced at her watch. He understood. 'You won't wait till I come downstairs again?' She shook her head and gestured to indicate that he shouldn't worry; she would see herself out.

She picked up her purse and sandals. When she passed the sun room, she paused. It wasn't like it mattered. It shouldn't matter to her, she reminded herself, and yet she couldn't just leave.

She stepped into the room. The grandmother's figure was frozen in the same position. She took two steps closer. No sound of breathing. She walked up to the chair and stood there for a moment. The eyes were half-open. Niharika touched the slack jaw lightly, waited for a few seconds and then pressed the edge of her palm over the lids. Then she ran out of the room, out the front door, and towards her car.

She was already sitting in the car when she remembered—it was the watchman's day off and the gardener was on duty in his stead.

Niharika resolved not to honk. She would manage. She could drive up to the gates, draw back the bolt, push one side of the gate open, drive the car out, push the gate shut again. There was nothing she could do about pushing the bolt back into place. But she wasn't going to honk for the gardener. She couldn't bear it, not now. But when the car reached the gate, he was already waiting there, dressed in full pants, a vest and an unbuttoned shirt.

Niharika did not look at him as she drove past and when she glanced in the rear view mirror, she saw that his eyes were also lowered. Even after her car had pulled away, he stood at the gate, head bent, staring at his own clay feet.

SANSKRIT

Ranbir Sidhu

It is past seven when Anu hears the key in the door and a moment later, Hari's voice calling from the hall.

'Don't move,' she shouts. 'Don't go anywhere.'

'I need to piss. I'm desperate.'

She appears, holding a camera in one hand and a silver cone party hat in the other. The camera is disposable. She picked it up in the city, when she left work early, afraid she wouldn't find their camera at home. It makes no difference that she is the one who puts everything away, she can never find anything.

'Put this on,' she says.

Hari waves the hat away with an arm draped with a black overcoat. He drops his briefcase against the wall.

'I need to piss.'

'Please, darling.'

'Make it quick.'

She straps the hat onto Hari's head and kisses him on the cheek.

'Happy birthday.'

She steps back and snaps a photo.

'Did the flash go?'

'Yes,' Hari says. 'Now ...'

'It didn't.'

'Fine, it didn't. You had your chance.'

Hari walks past her, leaving the coat in her arms.

'What happened?' she calls after him.

'Bomb at Grand Central.'

'An explosion?'

'No, just a scare. A bomb scare. The place was evacuated.'

The downstairs bathroom door opens but doesn't close. Hari enjoys taking a piss with the door open. It's more intimate, more married somehow. Anu thinks it's gross. She can hear him pissing.

'Whiskey and soda?' she asks.

'Sure.'

He is leaning against the doorjamb leading to the kitchen, his fly undone, the party hat still on his head.

'I needed that.'

'Here,' she says, handing him the whiskey.

'Kiss me,' he says.

'I have to change.'

'Change?'

'You didn't think I'd dress like this.'

'How do you dress?'

'You'll see.'

Hari takes a long drink and nods at the bottle. Anu refills his glass.

'And?' he asks.

'I'm not telling. It's a surprise.'

He winks. 'I picked up something too. Something special.'

'What?'

Hari reaches into his inside jacket pocket and produces a rolled-up Ziploc bag. Raising this over his head, he unfurls it with a snap of his wrist.

'Pot,' Anu says, bringing her face up to the bag. 'That's so cool.'

'Bolinas razorback. This is serious shit. Organic, hydroponic, the works.'

'Roll one, will you? I'm going to change. There's a couple burgers in the bag.'

Hari spots the Wendy's bag on the counter.

'Birthday dinner?'

'Go ahead, stuff your face. I'll be in the bedroom. No peeking.'

He takes a framed photograph down from the wall, an enlarged black and white showing his father as a young man standing in a lush Ludhiana garden, wearing a suit and tie and holding an umbrella, both hands on the handle, tip pressed into the ground, the way Steed would in *The Avengers*. He sets the photograph on the coffee table, taps out a portion of pot onto the glass, and begins to press it through his fingers, sorting out the stems. He pulls a packet of papers from his pocket, Big Bambi, purchased at the corner store on West 40th, where he picks up his morning coffee.

The phone rings as he finishes rolling the joint. He checks the caller ID before answering.

'Jack,' he says.

'I don't feel motion, Harry, I don't feel anything moving. Are things in motion? Are we moving?'

'There is motion, Jack. There is motion on several fronts.'

'I am walking inside a miasma. I am walking round and round in a vast circle. I'm going to walk and discover my own footprints one day. That's how I feel.'

'It's going around.'

'You're a funny man. You should do stand-up.'

'We're making an assault, Jack. Planning stages, there are ground forces, there are recon teams. We have radar up and active, we have infiltration. We are on the verge of initiating first contact. Penetration is imminent.'

'Henderson?'

'Hawthorne.'

'What are you doing right now?'

'I rolled a joint. I hope that's not against company policy?'

Hari lights the joint and takes a puff.

'Tell me, Harry. You don't have kids?'

'You don't know?'

'I know. I want to hear it from you.'

'No, Jack, no kids.'

'What does that mean?'

'Jack?'

'What does it mean not to have kids?'

'It's quiet. That's what it means. It's quiet and I get to fuck my wife on my birthday.'

'That's why I was calling. I wanted to wish you a happy birthday. I almost forgot. It's amazing. I think I am losing my way.'

'Thanks.'

'Do you have a copy of the latest *Cosmo*? If not, then *Marie Claire*. One of those.'

'The magazines?'

'Wives subscribe. It's a basic principle.'

Anu does, he knows, and as he turns to search the shelf below the side table he is stopped by what he sees resting before the framed photograph of Anu's mother. It is a penis. Nothing more and nothing less. It is dark, flaccid, sitting atop a pair of balls. He reaches out a finger and pokes it. It feels soft, just like his.

He pulls the stack of magazines out from the lower shelf and sorts through them on his lap.

'Harry? Do you have the magazine?'

'Hold on, I've got a situation.'

'What kind of situation are we talking?'

'Nothing for you to worry about. I have *Cosmo* here.'

'Good. Page 158. I need you to turn to page 158.'

As he turns the pages, he lays the rubber penis on his knee and stares at it, the dark, ribbed flesh, the curl of the shaft, the uncircumcised foreskin. It's not hard like a dildo. It's soft and it looks like the real thing, except the base is cleanly sliced and MADE IN INDIA is stamped onto it. It shivers when he moves his knee, it rocks back and forth when he raises and lowers it. It is almost alive and he has to fight an impulse to reach out and stroke it.

'There's an ad,' Hari says, 'and an article about that actress from Idaho.'

'Put your face in the ad.'

'The perfume ad.'

'Yes. Put your face in it. Close your eyes. Then open the flap and breathe in. Inhale. I want you to inhale deeply before you open your eyes.'

The perfume is called Homicide.

'I smell it.'

'Good. Now open your eyes.'

Hari sees a naked woman, maybe sixteen, full, long blonde hair, eyes shut, a look of ecstasy on her face. He takes another toke on the joint.

'She's fuckable,' Hari says. 'Uber fuckable.'

'She is Willomena von Stettin-Coburg, original euro-trash royalty.'

'Nice. What are we talking about, Jack?'

'Your birthday present. We have a company discount. One grand. For one grand she will give you a blow job. She doesn't fuck. No one. I've looked into it.'

'Jesus.'

'It's one hell of a blow job. Top-notch production values, five-piece band, singer, professional lighting. The full-on razzmatazz. You'll never look back. She'll change your life, you'll be a spoiled man.'

'She's good?'

'Better. Have Peggy set you up. I'll call you later.'

She lies snaking across the perfumed fold, on her side, head thrown back, breasts vivid, even a shadow of pubic hair visible. Hari thinks about her mouth, her mouth around his dick.

He hears Anu let out a cry.

'Honey?'

There is a long silence and he returns his attention to the woman in the magazine.

'Honey?' he calls again.

'Nothing,' she says from somewhere in the house. 'I hate India.'

'What is it?' He lifts the penis to his face. He holds it in the palm of his hand, level with his eyes, and shakes it, watching it wobble. A moulded jelly dessert, he thinks.

'They don't teach you how to wear one!'

'Wear what?' He brings the penis to his mouth, holds it up against his lips, slides his tongue along the rubber foreskin. How do women do it?

'Hold on.'

He stands and fits the rubber penis into his open fly and walks to the bedroom door. With every step it shivers like the real thing.

'Honey?' he knocks.

'Soon.'

He waits, a hand idly playing with his second cock.

Anu appears in the half-light of the hall.

'Get on your knees,' he orders softly.

'What?'

'Get on your knees and suck my dick.'

She is dressed in a silver and blue sari, awkwardly, nothing right about it but he can't say what fails, what is wrong. Before he can look closely, she is on her knees, her mouth around the rubber cock.

She pulls back, the penis in her mouth, and lets it fall. 'Oh god,' she cries, drops with her back against the wall.

'Oh god.' She looks up, laughing, at Hari. 'I hate you. I thought it was ...'

'Yes,' he says, getting down on his knees. She is beautiful in the half-light of the hall, in the disordered sari, the surprised grin on her face.

'Kiss me,' he says.

'Later.'

'What's going on?'

'I had to staple it. Staple it everywhere.' She is almost in tears. 'Look at me. I'm a disaster. I don't know how, I don't know anything. I'm supposed to be an Indian woman. This is what I'm going to teach my daughter. God, I hate myself. I can't do anything. Not anything.'

'Here.' He hands her the joint.

She takes a long toke, hands it back, and picks up the rubber penis. 'I couldn't resist. I saw it there today and I had to. You understand?'

'I'm flying,' Hari says. 'That's all. I'm flying.'

'You are. I want to know. Tell me everything.'

'I don't know what it means. I can't feel my arms.'

'Yes?'

'No, I mean I feel my arms. It's like.'

'Yes?'

'I feel my arms for the first time. It's like I never felt my arms before. These are my arms. I feel them.'

'That's wild.'

'They're so there. On my body. Like they're real. Like they're real and they're real at the same time. Like I think they're there and they are there. There they are.'

'You have arms.'

'I have arms.'

The telephone rings. The landline. He jumps but she stops him with a hand on his shoulder.

'I'll get it,' Anu says, taking short, unsteady steps, her legs caught in the tightly wound sari. She looks Japanese, a geisha in a kimono, gingerly carrying the rubber penis.

'Hello Mom,' she says.

'What time is it over there?'

'What?'

'The time. What time where you are?'

'The same time as you.'

'Oh.' Her mother lets out a laugh. 'I was talking to India. I got confused.'

'I'm busy, Mom. Is there something?'

'Nothing. Well, yes, something.'

'What?'

'Oh nothing. Maybe another time.'

'Okay. It's Hari's birthday. Do you want to say hello?'

'No, you tell him happy birthday.'

'I will.'

'Wait. Just one thing. Where does he carry his cell phone?'

'What?'

'Where does he keep it? In his jacket pocket or his trouser pocket?'

'I don't know. Why do you want to know?'

'I'm worried. You've been married for four years and nothing. No baby.'

'Yes, Mom, we're waiting. We're taking precautions. When the time's right. We've talked, I've told you this.'

'Tell him to be careful. Not to keep his phone in his pants. I read today it damages the male sperm. The radioactivity. It makes monster children.'

'Mom? Hold on.'

'What?'

'Another call.' She clicks on the other line. 'Hello?'

'Anu? Is that you, Anu?'

'Mom? Hold on, I'm on the other line.' She clicks back. 'Mom?'

'The sperm, Anu, Hari's sperm.'

'I've got to go. It's Hari's mother.'

'But I'm your mother.'

'She's Hari's mother.'

'I'm also Hari's mother.'

'And she's my mother.'

'I'll call you later. Don't forget, Hari's sperm.'

Anu lowers the phone and places a hand over the mouthpiece. 'Your mom,' she calls. Hari appears from the kitchen holding a whiskey, and makes a puking motion, then strangles himself with one hand and feints a fall to the floor.

'I think he must be in the bathroom,' Anu says. 'I'll tell him to call you.'

'What time is it there?' Hari's mother asks.

'Oh, just past eight.'

'It's five o'clock here. The sun is out. It's raining.'

'It's setting here.'

'Nothing like California. You don't know what you're missing.'

'Maybe one day.'

'What are you doing? A party?'

'No, nothing special. Dinner, maybe a movie later. We're boring people these days.'

'No, not yet. You don't have children yet. Then you'll be boring.'

'I know.'

'Well ...?'

'What?' Anu looks across at Hari and rolls her eyes. He is standing in the kitchen doorway, grinning, places the drink on the counter, and mimes a full blast from a machine gun, mouth silently screaming, 'Rat-a-tat-a-tat-tat!'

'What is it you two get up to? Just dinner, just a movie? Hari's father is waiting, I am waiting. We're in California and we're waiting. Everyone is waiting.'

'Yes, yes. The whole world is waiting. Look, Mom, I'll have Hari call you when he's down.'

'Oh no, don't trouble him, not on his birthday. Tell him I telephoned. He'll be happy to hear his mother telephoned.'

'Homicide?' she says after she places the phone down, the magazine open on the table before her.

He sings. 'Psycho killer, qu'est-ce que c'est?'

'Bedroom,' she says. 'Now.'

Hari's cell phone rings.

'Leave it,' she says.

'I can't,' he says. 'It's Jack.'

'Just one thing,' Jack says. 'A word of advice.'

Anu walks into the kitchen and finds the joint. She climbs up onto the counter, still holding the rubber penis, and places it in her mouth. He can see the staples, they are everywhere, lines of them along each fold, each twist of the sari. The whole thing is a mess, nothing like how a sari should look. Each time she moves, a new line of staples catches the light. There must be hundreds of them.

'Sure,' Hari says.

'Change your name. Shorten it.'

'This is about Hawthorne?'

'This is personal. Think of it as a birthday bonus.'

'What do you mean?'

'My name is Jack. Understand? One word, one syllable. That's American. Your name is Harry. Two syllables. Good men died to be free of that second syllable.'

'I'm Indian, Jack. Hari is an Indian name.'

'Chinese, European, same difference. We're talking American. We're speaking to each other in a country where no one gives a damn about that second syllable. Bob, Bill, Mike, John, Fred, Art, Jake, Zack. These are American names. I want you to choose one.'

'Now?'

'When you feel like it. There's no pressure. Myself, I see you as Dick. Jack and Dick. Dick and Jack. With a name like that, we might be partners one day.'

'Are you making an offer?'

'This is an opening. This is a potential first step. I like what you're doing with Hawthorne.'

'Thanks.'

'I'll call you later.'

'Dick,' Hari says. 'What do you think of Dick?'

'I love it,' Anu says, pulling the rubber penis out of her mouth.

'I'm flying,' Hari says. 'I'm on the moon.'

His shirt is off and both his wrists are handcuffed to the bed frame. The handcuffs are padded with felt. Anu is working on tying his legs when the doorbell rings.

'Fuck,' she says.

'Ignore it.'

'No. I'll see. It might be someone.'

She rises, confused. He watches her disappear in a constricted rustle of silk and staple.

'Mrs Kastenbaum,' she says, realizing she is talking loudly, trying to hide how stoned she is.

Mrs Kastenbaum stands in the doorway, a short, plump woman with white hair, holding a potted plant.

'It's a money plant,' she says. 'It brings you money.'

'That's kind, that's very kind. Thank you. How did you know?'

'Know what?'

'Hari's birthday.'

'Oh my goodness, no. What a coincidence. Is he okay? Did he make it home without a problem? I'm terrified just thinking about it. I'm still shaking.'

'Did something happen?'

'Nerve gas. They released nerve gas, I'm sure of it.'

'What are you talking about?'

'At Grand Central Station, underground. People are dying, they will die. They will choke on their bathroom floors. I know it.'

'It was a bomb scare.'

Mrs Kastenbaum blinks, looks at Anu closely, as if her eyes have been closed this whole time, as if suddenly, after many decades of being blind, she is miraculously given sight again.

'It's a sari,' Anu says.

'You stapled it.'

'I know ... I just—'

'I've never seen anything so ... so ...'

'Yes?'

'You dress like this every night?'

'Well, not ...'

'You Indians are deeply rooted people. I'm impressed.'

'It's just ...'

'I thought of you two as a modern couple, you know, drugs, parties, electrical devices, that sort of thing. Who knows? Adultery.'

'Yes.'

'It is so rare, people who take the past seriously, people who respect their parents, their mothers. No one respects their mothers anymore.'

'Yes.'

'Will you say something for me?'

'I don't understand you.'

'In your language.'

'In English?'

'No. In Sanskrit.'

'Sanskrit?'

'I've always wanted someone to say something to me in Sanskrit. I've never had the courage to ask.'

'No one speaks it.'

'No one?'

'It's for the gods.'

'Oh.' Mrs Kastenbaum turns to leave and stops. 'People are dying,' she says.

Hari's cell starts to ring the moment Anu enters the bedroom.

'Quick,' he says. 'See if it's Jack.'

'It's Jack.'

'Hold it to my face.'

She answers the phone. 'Here he is, Jack,' she says.

'Jack?'

'I'll make this quick,' Jack says. 'This is about Hawthorne.'

'Go ahead.'

Anu hovers over him, lit by candles on all sides, her hair falling down about his eyes. He is watching her the whole time he talks to Jack, her eyes, mouth, lips. Who is she? How did they marry? How did they meet? The past is oblivion.

'Stick him like a pig,' Jack says. 'Stick him and stick him hard. Up the ass. Do you hear me?'

'I hear you.'

'You'll get one chance with Hawthorne, maybe not even that. He has his mouth wrapped around Keppenmeyer's dick. He's sucking hard. You need to be aware of this. I want you to stick him in the ass and make the shit scream. I want to see shit flying out his mouth. Is your dick big enough for that?'

'My dick's big enough.'

There is a long silence.

'I am in the abyss, Harry. I am staring into the abyss. I am falling. It's a very long way down.'

'You'll be fine, Jack. We all will.'

'I like your attitude. It's a great reassurance. I don't know if it's enough. There are things you don't know.'

'Yes, Jack.'

'Remember. Hawthorne takes it in the ass. I'll call you later.'

Anu shuts the phone and drops it on the bed.

She says, 'One of these days, you're going to have to tell me what you do for that man.'

She is watching, she is looking at his face, at the shadows, the play of light caused by the candles.

'My feet,' he says. 'Tie my feet.'

'Wait. I want to say something, I want ...'

She loses the thread. For a moment she saw something, something vital and deep in his eyes, about herself, about him, about the two of them together. In a flash it is gone.

'I'm losing my mind,' she says.

'Not you too.'

'No, just ...'

'Yes?'

'Mrs Kastenbaum thinks we speak Sanskrit.'

'We don't?'

'No one does, darling.'

'Not even when we were little?'

'Don't ask me, I'm flying.'

'Tie my legs.'

'Which ones are your legs.' She falls forward onto his chest. 'Did you eat both the burgers?'

She licks his neck, up, across, to his ear.

'Tie me till it hurts,' he says.

She raises herself on her elbows and looks at him hard.

'Pig,' she says.

His cell phone rings.

'Hey Jack,' Anu says. 'Long time, no speakee.'

'Annie,' Jack says. 'I need Harry.'

'He's all tied up.'

'Darling,' Hari says. 'Hold it to my face.'

She shakes her head. 'Fuck you.'

'Jack,' he shouts. 'Ignore her. She's talking to me.'

She shuts the phone and drops it on the floor.

'Cunt,' he says.

'Prick,' she says.

'Fuck me,' he says.

'No,' she says.

The phone rings again.

'Hold it this time.'

She sticks her tongue out and holds the phone to his ear.

'Harry, that you?'

'I'm right here, Jack.'

'I'm having a crisis, Harry. You're the only man I can talk to about these things. The two of us share a natural affinity for order and a well-regulated life. We are blood brothers, we are kin of a higher order. I look upon you as my spiritual body double. I'll hire you to impersonate me in heaven one day.'

Anu bites his nipple and he stops himself from letting out a cry.

'Do you mind if I call you Dick?'

'Go ahead.'

'Okay, Dick. Don't you like the sound of that?'

'Sure. What's on your mind?'

'Could it be that I am not who I am?'

'What are you getting at?'

'Those movies, you must have seen them when you were a kid. Body snatchers, aliens with the power of mind control, top secret government experiments. Maybe I am an alien in my own body, maybe I am someone else entirely. I might be sitting right now in a room in Arlington, Virginia, and here is my body, walking around an office in midtown.'

'That's the movies. In the movies, no one's who he is.'

Anu is running her tongue along his throat, his chin, a foot playing over his crotch.

'That's an interesting idea, Dick. I'm impressed. But what about the one where Heston plays Van Gogh? Is he Heston? Is he the painter? Who is he, if he's not one or the other?'

'Jack?'

'Yes, Dick?'

'What are we talking about?'

'I'll tell you a story, Dick. I once put a loaded pistol up my first wife's cunt. It was my grandfather's gun. He carried it in the Great War. Then it was my father's. He carried it in the Second World War. Then it was mine. I pushed it up my wife's cunt one night and I told her I was going to kill her if she refused to give me a divorce.'

'What happened?'

'She said no. I pulled the trigger. I'm not kidding. The gun was loaded and I pulled the trigger. I don't know why I'm telling you this, Dick. I've never told anyone, not even my lawyer.'

'Did she die, Jack? Did you kill her?'

Jack says nothing.

'Jack?'

Anu releases one of Hari's wrists and brings his hand to the phone. She raises herself, first on all fours, straddling his body like a cat, the sari falling from her figure and across his chest, then is free of him.

'That's the beautiful thing,' Jack says finally. 'In all those years, that gun never once misfired. That was the one time it did. I tell you, Dick, I had the best sex of my life that night, the very best. It remains unequalled.'

Hari shoots her a look of alarm and she puts a finger to her lips and tiptoes out.

In the kitchen, all the way at the back of the cupboard over the microwave, she finds her stash of Dunhill's. Not even Hari knows about them. She pulls out a pack and matches and takes them outside, onto the concrete porch, and sits down in the cool night air. She can hear Hari calling after her.

She lights a cigarette, inhales deeply. It has been six months since she last smoked. The tobacco tastes stale, glorious, despite the high, it goes straight to her head.

Across the street she sees Mrs Kastenbaum at her kitchen window, face framed by bright yellow ruffled curtains. Her face is deformed and ugly and frightening. Her eyes are enormous insect eyes, staring through the window glass. It takes Anu a moment to realize Mrs Kastenbaum is holding a pair of binoculars to her face. The old woman lowers them and raises an arm and waves. She is wearing a gas mask, large and dark, the filter hanging from her face like a freakish nose.

The Bolinas razorback kicks in. It is sudden, like the drug has been puttering her along in second gear for miles and with one punch of the pedal shoots her up to fifth.

Everything transforms.

She looks up at the few stars, the sky is burning, it is on fire, stars are falling from the heavens. She is melting into the concrete. Everything is molten, the street, the houses, the whole city is a river of flames. She can see

Mrs Kastenbaum. The two large insect eyes are at her face again, hovering in the kitchen.

Anu wants to say something. She wants to tell Mrs Kastenbaum something desperately important. She tries. She opens her mouth. She forms the words. Nothing comes out. The words are stuck in her throat. They are not even words, they are sounds, the sounds people made before they could say anything.

She stubs out the cigarette, lights another. Inhales. The world is fire, she thinks, and tries to make a sound and fails. When she looks up, Mrs Kastenbaum is gone.

ABANDON

Shrimoyee Nandini

IT BEGINS BY ACCIDENT, or so I'd assumed. We are driving back from a party at a farmhouse, a little out of town. We have just started seeing each other.

'Stop, stop the car. Can you park here?'

I pull up. The highway is dark. She gets out of the car. 'Come with me.'

I follow her. She walks towards a construction site on the side of the road, and without a sideways glance, through the gap in its chain-linked gate. 'Where are you going?' I ask.

'Quiet. We have to be quiet.'

She circles around the building's perimeter. It looms over us. 'What are we doing?' I ask again. 'Do you need to pee? You can go here, no one's around. I'll keep watch.'

'No,' she says.

Then she walks into the building. I follow. She has an air of knowingness about her that is intriguing, but not entirely sure of itself. It is accompanied by a sense of stealth, a barely repressed arousal. We are in some sort of stairwell. It is dark as pitch. I stub my toe and swear. She hushes me again, turns on her cell phone, and begins to climb the stairs by its glow.

'Where is everybody?' I ask. 'Don't the labourers live here?'

'They've left. The bubble has burst, you know. No one will live here. It's all gone.'

'But ...'

'There are guards sometimes, not often. It's empty—all gone,' she says again, pre-empting my question.

We reach a landing. She stops and turns towards me abruptly. Our bodies collide. Her body feels like a shock against mine. 'This will do,' she gasps. Something overtakes us both in that instant—a crazy need for rutting. There is no other word for it. We claw the clothes off each other, and lunge at skin. I hike up her skirt, her thighs girdle me. I push her against a wall, brace my arms around her and enter her. She screams. I hold my hand over her mouth, and she bites down hard. Her grunts are feral as I fuck her. Her body is slippery with sweat. The cement of the wall grazes my arms and rubs her back raw. I can hear my heart pounding. It does not stop until we are back in the car, examining our bruises and love bites.

The next weekend, after some discussion of practical necessities (my car, her blanket, my condoms) we do it again. We leave the house past midnight, and look for deserted construction sites across the city—half built structures that fall some storeys short of the apartment blocks that they were intended to be. A few pillars, a floor or two, a reasonably navigable staircase is all we ask for. Walls are optional, but preferred, because of the shadows. She is right. Buildings such as these are not hard to find these days, if you know where to look. In some areas there are whole colonies of them, rising darkly from the roadside. Blank patches in the skyline, amongst the glowing domes and spires. The routine is simple. Park around the corner, check for guards and stray dogs, stroll casually but briskly into the building—me leading, her following a minute later. Climb to the top floor, or any floor, lay down the blanket in a likely spot, and fuck. Sex is always a frenzied, half-clothed, clench-fisted thing. A fierce fight, pressed down against the cold cement, or if the fancy takes us, up against a pile of sandbags.

At first we are tentative, groping our way around the innards of the half-built structures, holding hands. Later, as we grow more familiar with such places, we are more self-assured. 'We don't talk about sex in the same way anymore,' she remarks one day when we've been doing it for a few weeks. It's true. Our sex talk has bifurcated like our sex lives. We still use the old words to speak of the sag and bounce of sex in bed—the college slang of 'snog' and 'bonk'. But this other thing requires something altogether more forceful—nailing, we call it. Banging. Hammering. Pounding. Only 'fucking' sometimes successfully transitions between the two worlds. After the first few times of rapid in and out, we begin to take more time over it. We look wide-eyed at the sky through scaffolding and partially built ceilings as we fuck. Sometimes a blinking neon light sets the rhythm.

Afterwards, smoking a cigarette, we only talk of this time, and other times like this.

'Did I hurt you?'

'Was I too loud?'

'Do you like this view better than Avalon?'

We christen the sites in keeping with the prevailing naming conventions of high-rises. 'Primrose Heights', abandoned after the ninth storey for instance, is nestled between the fully occupied 'Dahlia Palace' (twenty-four storeys) and 'Tulip Towers' (thirty-two storeys). Sometimes, as in the case of our favourite building of all, 'Felicia', it is a rust-covered builder's board that announces what the stillborn is destined never to be named. We could not improve upon the lyrical quality of 'fellatio on the fourth floor of Felicia'.

As time goes on, we grow knowledgeable and more nocturnal. We learn the locations of the all night chemists, the petrol pumps, the chai wallahs, the bread-omelette guys, the cigarette sellers. We watch the night nurses, escorted by their protective entourage of whores, trudge across the railway over-bridge to work. We see gelled young men, lately released from revels, getting a late night snack, their car doors wide open, the music thumping. Sometimes people with suitcases try to stop us on lonely flyovers to hitch a ride. 'Where are they coming from?' she says. 'Why are they walking on the flyover? How did they get here?' A man slumped in a drunken stupor at the edge of a bus stop with his hands in his trousers, may elicit a puzzled, 'Look at this guy. Is he masturbating? Is he asleep?' Other than these occasional musings, for which she seems to require no response, a sort of quiet descends upon her on our night rides home.

After our excursions, we like to go to the 24x7 at the petrol pump closest to her house, ostensibly to buy cigarettes or chewing gum. There, under the fluorescent lights, all her quietness leaves her, and she turns boisterous. I wear an exaggerated look of long suffering while she goes up to the makeup trial counter and makes herself up, pouting and tossing her head. Her face painted every lurid shade, I drop her off at her place. I never stay the night. Instead, I wend my lonely way back across the city, occasionally stopping for the men with bags. They are usually coming from the bus terminal, and want to go to places on the far edges of the Ring Road. Places with names I can never quite remember the next day. I offer to drop them to what I hope is the closest point, and they always get into the car. They are usually too exhausted to speak much, and sleep while I drive. I never tell her about these hitchhikers. She sees the men as mysterious visitors from another universe who drop down onto flyovers at night with all their worldly belongings. Saying they are on their way to Kirtan Nagar will only disappoint her.

The first signs that we are not alone appear when we have been going to the buildings for six weeks. It begins with the discovery of an abandoned panty (pink, small, cheap) in a yet unnamed building. I conjecture it is students with no other place to go, or beggars—even they must fuck somewhere. At first she agrees with me, but she abruptly changes her mind and grows grim. 'A panty is not conclusive evidence of sex,' she says, and objects to the ease with which I have presumed such sexual abandon in an unknown woman. 'Perhaps some woman peed in her pants and needed to get rid of them.' Why she should brave four floors of tortured concrete to do so is moot.

'Or maybe it's a cross dresser, who uses this place to change into his work clothes?' I suggest.

'Perhaps a bird picked it off a line and dropped it here.'

A panty means nothing. Nothing at all. It is entirely innocent, she continues to insist. I, already tired of this argument, agree.

Three weeks later it is a condom wrapper. A week after that, a used condom. She says nothing as I carefully pick it up and throw it off the edge. We begin to leave accidental evidence of our own—an empty tube of KY, a button that comes loose from her shirt. When we return after weeks to the same spot the things have disappeared. But occasionally, some object is found where we left it, and we are inordinately pleased. A beer can I left on the second floor landing of 'Gardenia' turns up at another of our buildings, halfway across the city. I am certain it is the same beer can, flattened exactly as I had squashed it. This sets us off on a brief interlude where we gather the flotsam we find (an astrologer's business card, an empty pan-masala packet, a metro token, a matchbox) and leave it elsewhere on our next trip. My dashboard becomes a dumping ground of such debris. We stop doing this when a handkerchief I ferry to the roof of 'Verona' conveys itself back to the precise spot I'd picked it up two weeks ago. After this we feel compelled to let things be. We content ourselves instead with adding our initials to the others, lazily scraping the gravel and loose cement with the pointy end of a belt buckle or hair clip, in a post-coital moment.

Nonetheless, the mysterious moving of things, amusing at first, begins to make us increasingly nervous. Almost without noticing, we start going further afield, to darker places in more distant suburbs. Yet, the unmistakable signs of other people follow us. We grow more watchful, on the constant lookout for people like us. We imagine rustlings and whisperings, grunts and moans, everywhere. The buildings seem alive with the presence of fucking. Amidst the sounds of our own ragged breath, our hammering hearts, our strangely reverberating moans, we fancy that we hear other faint echoes, catch distant footsteps, glimpse unexplained shadows. Though we never meet a soul, we begin to wonder aloud if it is becoming too dangerous. We doubt ourselves, we dismiss our doubts, we guess and second-guess. On the days she believes in the existence of the 'others', as we call them, she is convinced the women are prostitutes without a place to see their johns. To disprove her, if only to myself, one day I walk across the railway over-bridge to see if a whore will suggest sex in a nearby building. Though several offer me their services, they all have rooms in lodges.

One day, we are in one of our in-between places—outdoors but not quite outdoors, on an almost-veranda, looking out at our city. The stadium lights in the distance give the sky the feel of twilight. I turn to say something to her and she kisses me. We stand there, slowly kissing, the occasional car passing below us. I run my hand over her breasts, my fingers scraping her nipples. She arcs herself and presses against me. I step back and watch her.

She pulls my t-shirt over my head and kisses my neck. The sudden air is cool, and my skin breaks into goose bumps. She turns, faces the wall and offers me her back. I kiss the hinge of skin on her nape, beneath her hair. Her ass is wedged tightly against me and rocking slowly. My knuckles trail her breasts, her sides, under her arms. She pushes harder against me. It's making me impatient, but I know she wants this slow. I want it slow too, but then I want it all. I turn her around, and kiss her stomach, and hover over the waistband of her jeans. I slide my hand in, undo them and pull them past her hips. I kneel in front of her and start to kiss the uncovered patch of skin on her thighs, between denim and cotton. She whimpers, parting her legs so that I'll put my mouth to her. 'What?' I ask, looking up. Then, I pull down her panties and lay tongue on clit. 'Oh good,' she sighs. Her legs won't hold her; her jeans are tangled around her knees. She falls towards me and braces herself against my shoulders, her breasts swinging, as she slides and squirms against my tongue, my mouth, my chin. As I continue to lick and suck her, I become aware that something has changed. She has turned strangely still and silent. I look up at her again, and she is gazing at something beyond the wall, behind my back. I stop. 'No. Don't. Don't stop,' she says, and pulls me deeper into her.

Afterwards, as we sit cross-legged on a gunnysack and share a cigarette, I see it too. The unmistakable glow of another lit cigarette a few metres away. It is held by a woman. Tall, grey-haired, perhaps in her fifties. She is dressed in what seems to be a white terry cot robe, the sort you get in five star hotels. She is wholly unperturbed at being seen by us, as if she were enjoying a quiet smoke on her own balcony, instead of on a hanging parapet suspended from the skeleton of a building in the middle of nowhere. She draws deeply on her cigarette and tosses the still-lit stub towards us in a slow, deliberate arc. As we watch, she undoes the sash of her robe. She stands there with it flapping around her for a minute, her breasts catching the halogen streetlight. Then she turns around and disappears into the dark. A few minutes later we hear a car pull away.

On the ride back, we are unusually talkative, describing endlessly to each other what it was that we think we have seen.

'A woman.'

'Definitely a woman.'

'Old-ish?'

'Yes.'

'Probably someone like us.'

'Not a construction worker or a student.'

'A smoker.'

'Driver of a car.'

'It could be your mother,' she laughs.

'My mother doesn't smoke,' I say.

'Well, then it could be mine.'

When we get to her place, she is restless. 'Come upstairs, for a bit?' she asks. I follow her up, but she hardly speaks to me once we're there. I leaf through a magazine. She smokes a cigarette on her balcony and says she is going to bed. I am at the front door when she turns to me and says, for the first time since our relationship began, 'Why don't you stay the night?' I lie down beside her on her single bed, but she tosses and turns constantly, growing sticky with sweat. Her room is too hot, she complains, she can't sleep. I wonder whether I should offer to sleep on the floor, but don't. After about half an hour, she goes to the bathroom and stands under the shower with all her clothes on. She comes back to bed shivering, curls away from me, and falls asleep almost immediately. I am awake for a long time, and leave for work before she wakes up.

After that night, other things become possible. Getting fully undressed, for instance, and sitting around afterwards naked in the emptiness, watching the passing headlights or whatever the view offers. In these quiet moments, the 'others' lose their menace. We become experts on the imaginary nightlife of abandoned construction sites. We gossip and catalogue the types: there are the Newbies, nervous and urgent, like we used to be. The Regulars, people like us. The Over-prepareds, yuppies with torches and rucksacks, what we are on our way to becoming if we don't watch out. There are the Students, of course, escaping hostel curfews. There is the Call-centre Crowd, sneaking a quickie in their 3 a.m. coffee break. The Professionals, the Solitaries, the One-offs, the Gay men, the Watchers. A whole army of silent watchers—alone, in pairs, in groups. I sometimes wonder what it would be like to come to one of these places unaccompanied and watch the lovers fuck. But I never do. Though I do finally ask her if she has done this with anyone else.

'Yes,' she says, 'once. With a random guy from college.'

When she tells me his name, it turns out I know him. 'Small world,' I say.

'Why does nobody do anything about us?' she asks, on one of our rides home. 'Surely it can't be that they don't know.'

'Maybe they're doing it too, whoever "they" are. Why does it bother you?'

'I don't know,' she pauses. 'Who are all these others?'

After this conversation, she frequently begins to voice anxieties about 'them' 'putting a stop to it all' 'sometime soon', though this imminent end only seems to make her want it more. I have begun to stay over at her place more regularly, but otherwise little changes between us. I always leave for work the next morning unsure where it is headed, or whether it will all end soon, as she portends.

One night, while I fuck her on the eighth floor of 'Laburnum', the walls begin to shake. A tremor runs through the floor. I lose my balance and fall. It takes me a moment to gather my wits, but she is already scrambling to get her clothes.

'It's falling,' she says, 'it's coming down.'

She drags me by the arm. The trembling has stopped, but there is a growing reverberation that sounds ominous. I hear the distant sound of glass breaking. We begin to run, still undressed. The pillar she was pinioned against seconds ago has cracks across it. We clamber across the floor, which is beginning to tilt.

'My phone. My phone,' I find myself saying.

'Fuck your phone,' she says.

There is a sound like continuous thunder. I am not sure if it is the building or the blood in my head. She is screaming constantly now, a shrill monotone. 'Are you hurt?' I want to ask but my throat is clogged. She pushes me roughly towards the stairs, which we begin to tumble rather than climb down. As we start descending the second flight, soft grey dust begins to fall like rain. A hailstorm of brick and mortar follows. In the middle of it, I feel her let go of my arm. There is a rush of air and the deafening sound of concrete crashing. I turn around and sense that the stair above me has disappeared—there is void where there should be wall.

Her voice calls out from above me. 'I'm stuck.' I jump, flailing my hands, hoping to touch something. 'My foot is stuck under this,' she says again, sounding oddly calm. I hear myself beginning to scream, still leaping and grabbing at air in my hands. 'You should go ahead,' she says. 'Get help.' But I remain, flapping, whirling, crazed and blind, losing my balance. The cement is still raining down, getting in my eyes and nose. A full minute later, after a series of grunts and curses, I hear her say, 'It's free. I think I'm fine. I'm going to jump, hold me,' and her naked body falls neatly into my arms.

I don't remember how we manage to clamber the rest of our way down. We reach the street still unclothed. She is unrecognizable, her face an ashen mask, her hair and eyelashes the grey of a much older woman. She is limping, her ankle sprained, perhaps fractured. Her nose is bleeding, and a red trail runs from her nostril to her mouth. She licks her lips, revealing an island of pink flesh surrounded by dust. 'Stress,' she laughs, 'always gives me nosebleeds.'

We've begun to walk away when the rest of the building comes down behind us with a roar. As we limp to the car, through the gloom and clouds of suspended dust, we see the others. Naked human forms covered in fine cement are crawling out of abandoned construction sites all around us. They lumber down the street in ghostly pairs. Some are holding each other, others are being dragged or half carried. After the deafening noise of the building, the street is eerily tranquil. A solitary man sits by the roadside, trying to put on his grey clothes. We do not stop or offer help. We drive back to her place still naked, still covered in cement.

Forty-nine abandoned buildings collapsed around the city that night. We watch the ambulances on television. A white handkerchief floats down the screen in an infinite loop, as we pick the grit and broken glass out of each other's skin and hair.

MOUTH

M. Svairini

SHE HAD A NAME, but tonight she would just be Mouth.

How delicious and perverse it felt to be addressed just by her gender, her primary genital area. Only a mouth. The outfit that Nikhil had sent her to wear emphasized that status. Mouth salivated as, naked, she stepped into the red neosilk bodysuit. Her feet slid into six-inch stilettos attached to the legs. She pulled the filmy material up her plentiful body, smoothing it tightly over the rolls around her hips and waist, then up over her breasts, defining them. The jumpsuit stretched so tight that it was nearly translucent in places. She loved the sexy look of expensive neosilk—harvested from the toxin-jacked-up silkworms of the blast zone formerly known as Kashmir, so strong that it would never rip. Her fingers wiggled into gloves, while built-in kneepads let her know the position she'd be expected to take for the evening, if she was lucky. The only opening was a hole in the hood, framing her dark, round, and, as she noticed in the almirah mirror, slightly flushed face.

She painted on her bright red lipstain, shuddering as the moist aphrodisiac gel touched the six sensitive neuro-crystals in her lips. They sparked and sparkled. Almost of its own will, her tongue responded by shifting against the insides of her teeth. She heard herself panting lightly as she licked the sweet t-spot on the roof of her mouth. Perhaps she should masturbate to orgasm, just to take the edge off so she could manage the hour-long ride to Nikhil's place in peace?

But then she looked at the clock: 19:45. The Metro station was only minutes away, but with the post-rush-hour crowds and in stilettos, she should give herself the extra time. She fumbled with the outfit's last piece: a triangle of red silk, with small golden hoops attached to two of its corners. Ah, earrings. One ring in each earlobe, and the ingenious veil fell just below her nose and across her mouth. The silk brushed against her lips so lightly that she felt naked. She would have to be careful of the wind that sometimes picked up when the trains came. She imagined a breeze lifting the veil, exposing her genitalia to everyone.... Stop it, she told herself firmly. But she was already wet, and she swallowed hard.

Mouth was old enough, just barely, to remember when people had lived up on the Surface, before the Emergency. These days a Metro ride was one of the only ways to catch a glimpse of Up There. Stepping into the station, she was captivated as always by the toxic red mists that swirled beyond thick translucent plexi walls, concealing an abandoned landscape once filled with homes and buildings. Post-humanity, she imagined apsaras and asuras copulating in the scarlet fog, swallowing and licking the constantly shifting shapes of one another's insubstantial flesh. Immersed in scenes half-real and half-imagined, at first she didn't realize that her fellow passengers on the train were staring at her.

The other riders looked away quickly, of course, and technically her dress was impeccable, she assured herself as she settled into a window seat. Her sex was covered, which was the important thing. Others wore far less than her: across the aisle a teenager sporting just a loincloth was nearly kickboxing in her seat, absorbed in a personal portable holo-game, while further ahead, two IT workers wore only aprons over their rear parts. But the fabric they wore was standard issue, thick enough to conceal their respective genitals ... not sensual and flimsy like the bit of red silk that barely covered her own hole.

And besides, they weren't mouths, as seventy-five per cent of legal prostitutes and ninety-nine per cent of illegal prostitutes were, according to the report Mouth had copy-edited that morning for the Executive. Of the four genders, mouths were the most likely to be arrested for crimes of perversity and solicitation; the most likely to drop out of school; yet ironically (she had nearly laughed aloud reading this line) the most likely to report 'high' or 'extremely high' levels of Life Satisfaction. Translation: mouths do it better.

But respectable mouths avoided the taint of perversity. At work she dressed like everyone else: loose-fitting salwar-kameez in a gender-neutral colour, headscarf wrapped just below her nose. In that quasi-uniform, no one was supposed to know if you were cock, pussy, ass, or mouth; all four genders were equal in the eyes of the law.

Somehow, though, everyone always knew. And Mouth could understand why restaurants had developed separate eating areas for mouths, why co-workers excluded her from friendly lunches. If a mouth ate in public, it was awkward for everyone, easily crossing the line into blatant exhibitionism. Soon after her own Sorting, when Mouth went out for kulfi with her friends as she often did, she'd found herself writhing in pleasure publicly as Chocolate Chip Chikoo overwhelmed her newly Enhanced organ.

The Enhancements, ironically, were supposed to create equality. A century ago, around the same time the toxins on the Surface had banished people underground and all reproduction to the laboratory, neuro-sexologists discovered a way to reroute most of the body's pleasure nerve endings to a primary area of choice or inclination. At first, only the rich could afford the new procedure. But when word spread, the masses rioted and politicians scrambled to be seen as progressive. When the FPP (Feminist Pleasure Party) took power, it was decreed that everyone deserved one focal erogenous zone, which offered a pleasure far greater than having sensation diffused throughout the body. A new system of Sorting was introduced, so now at puberty, you chose, based on preference or a demonstrated inclination, what you wanted your strongest pleasure centre to be. Within a couple of generations, the two genders had been replaced by four—cock, cunt, ass and mouth—and patriarchal pronouns were phased out. Everyone was now a *she*.

An older woman boarded the Metro and plunked awkwardly down in the seat next to Mouth. She wore just a long sequined lehenga in a bandhani pattern, and Mouth was fascinated by the rippling wrinkles of her pale teats hanging low on her torso, overlapping the waistband of the skirt by two or three inches. The woman noticed Mouth's gaze, and her eyes ran up and down Mouth's body in return, taking in the neosilk, high heels, kneepads, and finally resting on the delicate red veil. 'Headed for an exciting Friday night, are we, dearie?' she leered.

Mouth nodded politely before looking away. After a moment, the woman put her hand on Mouth's thigh, and Mouth did not stop her. Why should she? The groping felt good, and Nikhil had given no orders regarding her activities before the party. After a few moments, the woman took Mouth's hand and placed it on her own crotch, where Mouth felt a bulge that had not been there when the woman sat down. So, she was a cock. Mouth pulled back her hand, wanting to keep it legal; touching someone's primary genitalia in public was a crime.

The woman paused, uncertain if her fondling was still wanted, so Mouth parted her legs and inched forward slightly as encouragement, and soon she felt the woman's fingers stroking her tightly outlined labia. These were usually no more sensitive than her feet or hands, but tonight's anticipation had sensitized all of her skin, so the woman's ministrations excited her. No one could see Mouth's tongue flicking at that perfect spot on her palate.

Amid all the vibrations and sounds of the Metro, only the woman touching her felt the shudder that briefly overtook Mouth's whole body.

Out the train window, the fierce filthy air shaped itself into teeth, lips, bodies merging and parting like flames.

'Come in, my dear, we're just about to get started,' Nikhil said, kissing Mouth lightly over her lips, and grinning as the surprise contact through the thin material made Mouth gasp. Nikhil looked at her closely, taking in her flushed cheeks and glassy eyes, after-effects of her orgasm on the Tube. 'But it looks like you've already gotten a head start, am I right?'

Mouth nodded, and Nikhil made her describe the encounter with the woman on the Metro in detail as they walked downstairs to join the others. 'And you didn't say a word to her, not even to say thank you?'

'She got off the train right afterward,' Mouth said defensively.

'What a nasty little girl you are,' Nikhil said.

They entered the party room, and a tall person Mouth did not recognize, with electric blue dreadlocks and a very young face, engaged Nikhil in a deep, tongue-thrusting kiss. 'Who have you brought for me, Nikki darling?' she asked, stepping back to examine Mouth. Her eyes raked over every curve, lingering at last on Mouth's veiled genitals. Mouth felt self-conscious, objectified, and desperately hoped the girl-woman was pleased with her.

'Yummy,' the woman said, licking her bare pink lips. Mouth felt like a sweetmeat about to be devoured. 'Shall we get on with it then?' Others began to gather, and Mouth took the opportunity to study the scene.

Nikhil was a cock whose prominent position in the judiciary entitled her to more credits and larger living quarters than anyone else Mouth knew: a split-level apartment that took up three whole floors of a housing shaft. The unit's middle floor was the best place for a social event of this sort, since any sound would be buffered from the neighbours. Internal walls had been demolished, creating a huge room that managed to seem sparsely furnished despite a king-sized canopy bed in one corner, a baroque plum-and-gold sofa set, various fetish equipment and bondage devices, and a marble fireplace around which the guests clustered. Mouth saw that the other two guests were dressed almost like her: neosilk jumpsuits colour-coded by gender with built-in stilettos, kneepads, and convenient holes. It was obvious what their names were, at least for tonight: Ass, with a pretty orange dupatta covering her rear, and Cunt, wearing a diaphanous purple thong that was already soaked. Cunt must have had an eventful trip here, too, though she didn't look quite as satisfied as Mouth.

Nikhil and the unknown woman made up the rest of the group. Their outfits were black, made of a flowing chiffon, beautifully tailored and flattering. Nikhil wore a longish kameez over churidar pants, the stranger a sari whose blouse displayed her impressive cleavage. They would not have been out of place at an office party or evening function. In short, they were not dressed like whores, with their genders on display; they were clearly the Madams of the evening.

'Time for the icebreaker, isn't it, Nikki darling?' the woman said.

'Almost, my dear,' Nikhil replied with an indulgent smile. 'First let me do the introductions. In case anyone's blood is already flowing far from her brain, I'll state the obvious: Cunt, Ass, Mouth.' Nikhil gestured at each of them in turn, grandstanding as if hosting a much larger gathering, and then put her arm around the unknown woman's waist. 'And this lovely creature is Aurora Arizmendi Azim. That's Azim Madam to you lot, and you can call me Nikhil Madam. Your safe word for the evening is "pakora", although I doubt you'll need it; Azim Madam prefers to manipulate you with pleasure, rather than pain, which I hope will not disappoint any of you too much. Now, Mouth, go to the bar refrigerator and bring out the bucket of ice. You two: strip.'

Mouth was conscious of rustling behind her as everyone followed orders. She was slightly jealous; was Nikhil going to make her serve the drinks while everyone else got to play? The ice cubes were fashionably shaped into cylinders about an inch in diameter and four inches long, making a lovely display in the silver bucket, which was engraved with Khajuraho-like scenes of copulation. When she returned, she was surprised to see that the others had removed only the flimsy fabric over their genitals, keeping the jumpsuits on.

Nikhil took the ice bucket from her and said, 'You, too.'

Grateful to be included, Mouth quickly undid her earrings and removed the veil, revealing her painted, crystalline, throbbing genitals for everyone to see. But she soon forgot her self-consciousness as she admired the view:

Cunt had three sets of visible labia, each unfolding out from each other like the petals of a rare lotus, in various shades of pink and purple that seemed only slightly colour-Enhanced. Her clitoris, however, was bright magenta, at least a centimetre in diameter, and perfectly round as a button, with a large neuro-crystal pulsing in the very centre. It had no hood. Smaller crystals were sprinkled plentifully throughout the folds, in a v-shaped pattern that seemed to waver and wink at the room. Her entire vulva glistened with moisture, which dribbled out from the innermost folds in uneven rivulets escaping down her inner thighs. Mouth felt her salivary-erecto glands shift into overdrive as she contemplated licking up those tiny streams, following them to their kund deep within.

Then Nikhil made a sort of swirling-fingertip gesture toward Ass, who immediately turned around and touched her toes, displaying large, creamy buttocks covered in intricate mehndi designs that pointed toward an iridescent hole. Her ball sack and small penis, hanging down from the front, were also visible, though tightly encased in her orange latex outfit. An ass's Enhancements were mostly internal, and Mouth wondered what qualities had gotten Ass invited to this exclusive soiree. Taste? Capacity? Some sort of special neuro-sensations for one who penetrated deep inside?

'Part your lips, Mouth,' Nikhil said, which was easy to do, as she was almost panting already. 'You aren't allowed to let your lips touch each other for any reason this evening. Like the other two, your fuckhole is to be open to us at all times. Is that clear?'

Mouth nodded. 'Answer out loud,' Azim Madam commanded.

'Yes, thank you,' Mouth said, pausing as she tried to figure out how to say *Azim Madam* without closing her lips; 'Azi' ada,' which made everybody laugh.

'Oh, this is going to be very amusing!' Azim Madam said, clapping her hands with glee. 'Let's make her say lots and lots of sentences! Say "My Madam makes my mouth water".'

'Eye ada akes eye outh otter,' Mouth said, somewhat miserably, drawing another peal of childish laughter from Azim Madam and an amused, sadistic grin from Nikhil; no, Nikhil Madam, she corrected herself in her mind. It would not do to make that mistake out loud.

'Icebreaker, icebreaker,' chanted Azim Madam impatiently. How old was she, anyway? It was impossible to tell, though Mouth knew Nikhil, who was in her fifties, preferred mature women. At thirty-three, Mouth was one of the youngest women in Nikhil's circle. The others seemed to be at least in their forties, as far as Mouth could tell.

Nikhil addressed the three submissives, 'As a sort of icebreaker game—well, it'll be more of an ice-melter, na?—you will put on a show for us. We were going to have you wrestle for it, but I think there's an easier way to decide who goes first. Don't you, my dear?'

Azim Madam cocked her head quizzically.

'One of our guests has already had an orgasm this evening,' Nikhil explained. 'So I think she should service everyone first, before she gets another one.'

'It's only fair,' Azim Madam agreed. Mouth groaned inwardly.

'And Cunt looks more than ready for hers, don't you think, my dear?'

'But perhaps we should make her wait longer?'

Cunt, who had been looking hopeful, pressed her lips together. This reminded Mouth to keep her own mouth open, and as she listened to the Madams banter about the fate of their poor submissives, she licked her lips unconsciously.

Azim Madam caught the gesture. 'Our little Mouth is quite impatient, isn't she?'

'On your knees,' Nikhil said, and snapped her fingers, pointing to a spot on the floor. Mouth crawled to the centre of the circle, knelt in front of the Madams with her hands upturned on her thighs, and breathed deeply, enjoying the sense of relief that submission always brought her: from now on, nothing would be up to her.

Finally, they decided that since Mouth had already come, and Cunt was exhibiting over-eagerness and generally whorish behaviour, obedient Ass would get the first turn. The game was this:

Mouth would take a rod of ice between her lips. This itself would be excruciating, since her sensitive genitals were already swollen and overheated. She would use the ice-dildo, as well as her own lips and tongue, to service each of her co-submissives in turn. If the woman came close to orgasm, she could beg the Madams for release, and they would decide if she deserved it. If she failed to climax before the ice-rod melted, she was out of luck, and Mouth would be ordered to move on to someone else.

Mouth, whose genitals would be receiving more stimulation than anyone else during this game, was not allowed to come. She would only be allowed to beg for permission after everyone else in the room—including the two Madams—had had an orgasm. Therefore, it was in her best interests to bring everyone to climax as rapidly as possible.

Ass was told to get on all fours for the game, while the Madams settled into a wide loveseat with Cunt between them. They strummed Cunt's labia casually, making them flutter open and closed. Cunt was already letting out small moans as Mouth knelt on the floor behind Ass. The bucket of ice was next to Mouth, and she bent over and picked up one of the rods in her mouth. The ice shocked every nerve ending. It slipped, Azim Madam tsk-tsked, and Mouth tried again, using her teeth this time to hold it steady. As the frozen tip brushed against her palate, her t-spot fired with pain. Mouth wanted to push it out of her orifice and into Ass's hole as quickly as possible.

But Ass was tight, and to relax the sphincter, Mouth had to take the ice deeper in her throat and then work the asshole with her tongue. As the ice shrank between her hot lips, she swallowed and managed to work her tongue an inch or so into Ass's hole.

Ass moaned with pleasure and pushed back toward her to get deeper penetration. Mouth braced herself, then reorganized her tongue to push the rod inside Ass's warm, dark orifice. The Madams cheered encouragement, which Mouth heard in a rather muffled way over the sound of her own slurping. Suddenly the frozen rod slipped out of her grasp, as Ass's hole suctioned it deeper. Mouth let her tongue follow the pathway and lapped at the shallow insides of the hole, her sensitive taste buds picking up tones of citrus that reminded her of one of the enemas her very first ass lover had used, way back when they were still in Enhancement Phase. Ass's sphincters—she seemed to have at least seven—were pumping Mouth's tongue, sucking her in. 'Please,' Ass cried, and Mouth guessed the now-thin sliver of ice was pushing up against and stimulating other Enhancements further inside.

'Is the ice still there?' Azim Madam asked Ass suspiciously.

'It is, please Madam, please I promise, but it's melting, please may I come for you, oh oh oh—'

Ass's pungency was ripe and earthy, and Mouth's olfactory and gustatory nerves were sending desperate signals to her brain about the necessity of coming, sooner rather than later. She ignored them and tried to focus on matching the rhythm of Ass's backward thrusts, working her tongue harder, faster, deeper. She was rewarded with a fresh round of 'oh-oh-oh-oh-oh!' from Ass. The last bit of ice puddled to water, but Mouth decided to keep going, hoping that Ass might not notice or in any case would not complain. 'Plee-ee-ee-ee-ease!' screamed Ass, her voice cracking with desperation and need, which apparently pleased the Madams.

'Now,' said Azim Madam, and Ass came, releasing a mosambi-lime secretion and convulsing around Mouth's tongue in a series of contractions so powerful that it took every ounce of Mouth's willpower to stop her own orgasm.

She pulled out, exhausted, and sat back on her knees. Ass turned around and sat next to her, and they leaned on each other for a moment. Mouth was surprised at how emotional she felt toward Ass: proud and tender and grateful all at the same time. She rested her head on Ass's shoulder and closed her eyes.

'Thank you, Madams,' Ass said softly, after a moment.

Mouth sat up and opened her eyes. 'Thank you, 'ada's,' she echoed, meaning it. Azim Madam caught her eye and grinned, then blew her a slow sultry kiss that made Mouth flush all over, hungering to feel those long soft fingers, not just air, caressing her lips.

Cunt's extravagant vulva was only the surface of a series of gorgeous nymphae that unfolded, layer after countless layer. As Mouth thrust the ice inward, following it with her tongue, she felt like a deep-sea diver entering the world's most intricate sea anemone. When the crystals in her lips touched the ones embedded in Cunt's labia, electric impulses of pleasure surged through her entire body—and Cunt's, too, by the sound of her moans and pleas. There was plenty of ice, so Mouth left it protruding and moved upward to Cunt's prominent clitoris, swirling round and round it with her tongue, savouring the salty-sour taste, then seizing it with her whole mouth and pressing lightly with her teeth. Cunt was begging, thrusting, pleading, screaming about her need to orgasm, but Azim Madam just laughed.

'No, no,' she said, and Mouth heard that gleeful little clap again, 'this is far too much fun! Let's not let her come, darling?'

Nikhil must have agreed, and Mouth could tell that if she continued tongue-fucking Cunt's clitoris—now swollen to almost twice its size, looking more like a diamond-studded cervix than a clit—the poor submissive would be unable to help herself. She didn't want to get Cunt in trouble, so she pulled back and went searching through Cunt's delicious folds for the orifice again. Her tongue found the ice-rod, greatly diminished, and manoeuvred it upward to where she thought Cunt's g-spot would be. Cunt's moans grew increasingly guttural, the ice shrunk to barely a sliver, and still the Madams seemed determined to deny Cunt her pleasure. Mouth wondered what the punishment would be for coming without permission. Should she try to force an orgasm anyway, to ensure her own reward sooner rather than later?

Within seconds, the question was moot, as Cunt screamed 'pakora' and then a flood spurted all over Mouth's face. She pulled out and shook her head in surprise; Cunt's briny juices had even gotten in her eyes, and she wiped them with the back of her gloved hand before sitting back.

Nikhil was on her feet, and furious.

'How dare you,' she said, standing over Cunt. Cunt, still shuddering from the giant orgasm, began to sob and apologize all at once.

'I'm sorry Madam, Madams, oh, I'm so sorry,' she sputtered.

'Mouth, move,' Nikhil ordered without looking at her, and Mouth crawled away, barely remembering to take the ice bucket with her. She was over-stimulated, high from smelling and swallowing both Ass's and Cunt's juices, and terrified by the tone in Nikhil's voice, which continued, 'That is *not* the appropriate use of a safeword. How dare you use a precaution designed to care for your well-being to justify your own woeful lack of self-control!'

'Madam, I couldn't help—' Cunt began again.

'Shut up, you disobedient slut,' Nikhil said. 'My dear Aurora, how are we going to punish this misbehaviour?'

'How does she respond to pain?' Azim Madam asked.

Mouth tried to meet Cunt's gaze, to show she hadn't deliberately set the other submissive up for failure. But Cunt's eyes darted between the two tops as Nikhil replied to Azim Madam: 'She likes pain. It makes her come even faster.'

Ass smiled, and Mouth couldn't help grinning a little, too; apparently, they could both relate.

'Ah well then,' Azim Madam said, sounding slightly relieved, 'that won't do. Come here, naughty Ass.'

Mouth cuddled next to Ass on the loveseat and watched as Nikhil and Azim Madam quickly designed a tableau for Cunt's punishment: Cunt was on her knees, hands bound behind her by a length of rope that hooked to the ceiling. Her face was buried in Ass's lovely crack, while her own asshole was ploughed by Azim Madam wielding the largest of several dildos that Nikhil had pulled from a drawer and offered her. Neither end would give Cunt much satisfaction, as her gorgeous vulva was dangling untouched; nor could she control her own movements. A few drops of moisture dripped from Cunt's pussy onto the floor. Mouth was captivated by the sight of Azim Madam's soft breasts heaving as she plunged the dildo in and out of Cunt's asshole, ran her short fingernails along the submissive's back and smiled wickedly when Cunt writhed at her touch.

Nikhil grabbed one of Mouth's nipples and pushed her head toward the largest and loveliest member that Mouth had ever had the pleasure to know. It never failed to delight her, as well as scare her a little by its size: fully erect, it was at least twelve inches, three inches around, in the same lustrous olive colour as the rest of Nikhil's skin.

Mouth reached for the now mostly melted ice bucket, but thankfully, Nikhil shook her head no. Apparently only the submissives needed ice to break them. So Mouth placed her hands behind her neck, as she knew Nikhil preferred, and began licking the bulbous, mushroom-shaped head with swift, spiralling strokes. Nikhil grabbed Mouth and yanked her closer. Suddenly she had more dick than she could handle. She relaxed her jaw to open wider, and was rewarded with the first drops of Nikhil's fluid on the Enhanced taste glands in the very back of her throat, specially biodesigned to savour semen or simulated semen. Mouth grunted with pleasure as she sucked the wonderfully bitter-slick pre-cum from Nikhil's tip. She didn't care about the blood pounding in her head from lack of air; this fullness was the sensation she craved most, and if she had been able, she would herself have been pleading for an orgasm.

She could hear Cunt's frustrated moans and Ass's mounting cries. Nikhil pounded into Mouth's throat deeply, again and again. Just as Azim Madam ordered Ass to come, Nikhil ejaculated, bucking so hard that Mouth was thrust back several inches, and had to catch herself with her hands on the floor. 'Don't swallow,' Nikhil said just in time, so she tilted her head back, kept her lips open, closed her throat and let the thick warm nectar bathe her swollen taste buds.

Her mouth felt hot, fiery, as though her cells had been compensating for each round of ice by generating more and more heat. She rested for a moment, back arched, eyes closed, and when she opened them she could see the rearrangement of positions. The party was like a perverted game of musical chairs, she thought, except some people didn't get chairs. For some reason she found this idea hilarious, and started laughing, then sputtered and began to choke on her mouthful of cum. Nikhil pounded her on the back and wiped her lips, leaving them tingly. 'Okay now?'

Mouth nodded, sobering up a little. The room seemed very bright. Her whole body was pulsing with need, and her hole felt raw, hot, and terribly empty. She felt suddenly fragile, and wondered whether she was going to cry. 'I' sorry I didn't kee' the cu' in 'y 'outh, 'ada',' she said, but she had no idea if she was intelligible. Nikhil pulled Mouth up onto her lap and let her rest against her shoulder. 'Thank you, 'ada',' Mouth murmured, eyes closed, and felt Nikhil stroke her cheek gently. She let herself drift in a comforting sea of sensation.

After Mouth had calmed down, Nikhil thrust her forward with a hand between the shoulder blades so that her breasts jutted toward Azim Madam, now sitting on the loveseat next to them. Cunt was still tonguing Ass's opening, and Ass had apparently been given license to orgasm and was doing so over and over again. Cunt was not; clearly, she was going to pay for that first orgasm for a long time.

Then Mouth forgot all about poor Cunt as Azim Madam turned and leaned in toward her, blowing sweet breath laced with cardamom and cloves onto her lips. Mouth shivered, and Azim Madam laughed. 'Are you enjoying the party, my little Mouth?' Azim Madam asked.

'Yes, 'ada',' Mouth said. She wondered whether the beautiful, girlish woman was a cunt, ass, or cock.

'Say the whole sentence,' Azim Madam said, pouting like a spoiled schoolgirl. She all but stamped her foot.

'Yes thank you 'ada', it's a 'ery nice 'arty,' Mouth said quickly, and was rewarded with a cruel, pleased smile.

'Do you hear that, Nikki?' Azim Madam said. 'We throw an airy nice arty.' Nikhil laughed, and Azim Madam continued her interview. 'And are you very sleepy, my little Mouth?'

Mouth shook her head. 'No, 'ada', I' not slee'y.'

'Ah, but your jaw must ache, at least a little.'

As she said it, Mouth realized it was true. 'Yes, 'ada', 'y jaw does ache, 'ut—' she paused, not knowing if she was allowed to do more than answer the direct question. Azim Madam nodded, so she continued. 'I 'ant to 'lease you, 'ada'.'

'Ahh, such a sweet little slut,' Azim Madam said. 'You will please me, don't worry. Now just relax. You don't have to do anything right now, understand?' Azim Madam stroked her cheek softly.

'I think so, 'ada',' Mouth said, a little confused by the sudden gentleness.

Azim Madam ran her fingers along Mouth's lips, circling each of the six neuro-crystals in turn before tapping it directly, which caused Mouth's nerve endings to fire wildly. A mouth's standard Enhancement at puberty involved two neuro-crystals: one on the upper lip, one on the lower. They served as focal points for the pleasure nerves of the body, as well as for easy gender identification. The crystals were the last phase of Enhancement, and once you received them, your gender was set and you wore a mouth covering at all times in public. Mouth remembered her own 'graduation' fondly; although she had been wearing a veil for months before, she felt a special thrill on the day she *had* to wear it.

Years later, when she'd landed the job at the Executive and learned the exact amount of her new salary, she had gone out and bought the four new crystals on credit. They had been well worth the eight months of reduced rations it had taken her to pay them off. 'These are very pretty,' Azim Madam said, tapping them again, watching Mouth writhe. 'Very sexy.'

'Th-thank you, 'ada',' Mouth managed, though she was nearly nonverbal with longing. Her neuro-crystals had never been teased so deliberately, and on the heels of what felt like hours of delayed gratification, her synapses were about to go into overload.

But Azim Madam was not done. 'Show me your tongue,' she said.

Mouth poked the tip of it between her lips. Azim Madam grabbed it between two fingernails and pulled, sending a wave of pain ricocheting to Mouth's brain and forcing a loud 'aah' from her throat, which Azim Madam ignored.

'Two extensions of the intrinsic muscles, I think, and—let's see—one, two, three tongue crystals?'

Mouth nodded, gasping. A typical mouth's tongue had no extensions, just the severance of the fraenulum that gave the illusion of greater length. Mouth's expensive tongue, when fully unfurled, was about twice as long as an un-Enhanced tongue. Over the years, lovers had given her the extra neuro-crystals: one at the tip, useful for stimulating deep inside an ass; one in the centre, which added pleasure to almost every kind of licking, from lollipops to pussies; and one in the back for deep-throating. Nikhil had paid for this last one, and used her over and over in the first weeks afterward, plunging deeply and joking that Mouth had to 'make payments' for the jewel. Mouth was only too happy for the trade.

Apparently done with her inspection, Azim Madam let go of Mouth's tongue, leaving it to dangle limply before Mouth recovered her senses enough to draw it back in. 'Now I'm going to fuck you,' Azim Madam said. 'You are not to lick, kiss, suck, bite, or do anything at all with your fancy little Enhanced twat. You are my hole, nothing more. Is that clear?'

'Yes 'ada',' Mouth said. She was breathing hard with anticipation.

'Get on the floor and close your eyes. Hands behind your neck.'

Mouth scrambled out of Nikhil's lap to obey, eager to find out at last where Azim Madam's pleasure centre was. She had not realized it, but knowing a lover's gender was so basic, so key to understanding how to please her, that being deprived of that information made Mouth feel even more helpless. She kneeled, blind, genitals wide open, breathing. If she was to be a hole, Azim Madam most likely was a cock, she thought; although with various double-ended pleasure toys, asses and cunts could fuck a mouth quite nicely, too.

She heard a rustling in front of her, on the floor. Perhaps Madam shedding some clothes? But what she felt next surprised her: the Madam licking the outer corners of Mouth's lips.

Kissing between casual sex partners, while not taboo, was unusual, especially with a mouth. Even after more than a year of trysts, Nikhil rarely kissed her on the lips, except as a kind of tease.

But Azim Madam was kissing her lips directly now. Here was a new kind of torture, more sadistic than clamps or slaps: not to obey every cell in her body demanding that she respond to such direct stimulation. She was a hole, she told herself firmly; my Madam's fuckhole. She would endure this foreplay, she would not come, she would obey.

Azim Madam slipped her tongue inside Mouth's lips and explored the gumline, running her tongue over the bottom teeth, the top teeth, pausing at the sensitive t-spot and lapping it until Mouth was moaning aloud, clenching and unclenching her fists behind her neck, even thrusting her pelvis forward, as if that would somehow help. It wasn't her turn to come, not until Azim Madam had, but if this kept up she was going to find herself in poor Cunt's position.

But Azim Madam moved on; that is, in. Deeper. As her lips enveloped Mouth's entire opening, something sparked, and Mouth opened her eyes with shock. Azim Madam's mouth was locked over hers, and she was staring right into Mouth's eyes, waiting for her to process the sensation. Azim Madam had neuro-crystals embedded, not on the outside of her lips, but just inside: a dozen of them, at least, judging from the way Mouth's own crystals were going crazy.

Azim Madam was a mouth.

Mouth had no opportunity to consider this further, because suddenly her hole was full, and being ravaged more exquisitely than ever before. Azim Madam's tongue penetrated deeply and then rolled upward to scrape Mouth's hypersensitive palate. The foreign tongue seemed to have numerous little crystals hidden on its undersurface. And then it felt as though two tongues were in her, twisting around, now grabbing her tongue and tugging at it, now prodding at her taste-glands. One part of the split tongue went deep into her throat and seemed to widen and grow almost to the size of a long narrow cock. The other curled upward and jostled her t-spot. The Madam fucked her until she was sobbing, and then, just as Mouth was sure she could stand it no longer, she felt a flood of warm saliva fill her. Her first thought was that she had come without permission, but then she tasted cardamom and cloves, and realized the Madam had ejaculated in her mouth.

Azim Madam withdrew her tongue—tongues? what *was* she?—with a slow, torturous, spiralling motion. Mouth looked down, hypnotized, as one half of the Madam's tongue lightly licked Mouth's lower lip. The other licked her upper lip, teasing her even as it left her empty, gaping, needing. The tongues came together and returned to Azim Madam's mouth, which now expressed a relaxed, rather smug smile.

Mouth found she could hardly breathe, let alone speak. Her breath was shallow and loud; her heartbeat was louder still. Drool and cum dripped from her lower lip, and she was powerless to stop it, fearing that one more lick, even a slight motion of her tongue, would send her soaring across the threshold. She felt a wetness on her cheeks, and realized tears were streaming from her eyes. As if from a great distance she heard someone else begging to cum, permission being granted; the unmistakable sounds of orgasm filled the room once more. Mouth closed her eyes, and Azim Madam took her in her arms.

After a moment—too brief—Azim Madam shook Mouth off, stood up, smoothed her sari, and took her seat on the sofa again. Her full lips were moist and swollen, but without the telltale crystals on the outside, no one could have identified her as a mouth, even now. Mouth wondered what kinds of Enhancements these were, and how Azim Madam had been allowed to wear them concealed, and if there were others like her—though really all she could think about was the ache in her lips and palate, and her desperate, throat-deep, all-consuming need to orgasm.

'Thank me,' said Azim Madam. She was watching Mouth with keen, dark eyes. 'And tell me how that felt to you.'

Mouth arched her back trying to get enough air in her lungs for a deep breath, trying to calm herself enough to reassemble phonemes into words, sentences. She looked up at Azim Madam, marvelling at how beautiful she was, and blurted out, 'I lo' you, 'ada'.'

Azim Madam raised an eyebrow. 'Does she love everyone who fucks her silly?' she asked Nikhil.

'She's never said it to me,' Nikhil said, laughing. 'You must have made an impression, my dear.'

Mouth felt humiliated, but she did not regret her passionate words, even as Azim Madam looked at her and said coolly, 'What an interesting creature.' The Madam smiled slightly, as if enjoying a private joke. Mouth felt pinned by her eyes, unable to move or look away, and wanting only to stay locked in that gaze forever.

Nikhil said, 'It's your turn now, Mouth. Which of us would you like to decide how you get to come?'

Azim Madam turned away—a mercy, since it broke the trance. Mouth lowered her eyes and tried to think. After being denied decisions all evening, it was confusing to be asked to choose now. Her heart and nerve endings all wanted Azim Madam, there was no question about it; but she felt a loyalty toward Nikhil.

''lease 'ada's, 'atever you decide?' she tried.

Nikhil leaned down and slapped Mouth's right cheek, hard. Azim Madam followed suit with her left.

'We *decided* to give you a choice, my precious Mouth,' Azim Madam said, and Mouth's heart leaped at her use of the possessive. *Yes, I am yours*, something in her said, something that made her realize that in all of her years of submission, she had only been playacting. *Own me*, she wanted to tell her.

But Nikhil was staring at her. 'Hurry up and choose,' she said finally. 'You're not the only slut here we need to supervise.'

Mouth didn't want Nikhil to think badly of her; she felt a surge of gratitude to Nikhil for all the times they had shared together, and for inviting her tonight in the first place. ''lease 'ada' Nikhil,' she said finally, and Nikhil patted her lap.

Mouth climbed up, suddenly eager. A good finger-fucking by Nikhil and the release of an orgasm would be just what she needed to get her emotions under control.

But as Nikhil positioned her—sitting sideways again, hands twisted into prayer position behind her back, breasts thrust forward—Mouth found she was looking directly at Azim Madam. Again, she couldn't tear her eyes away from that dark, intense gaze; oh, and those full, ripe lips ... which came closer. And then she was in heaven, because Azim Madam was kissing her again. Could this even be called kissing? She didn't know; it was more intense than any kind of fucking she had ever experienced. Then the Madam pulled back.

'I'm guessing she could come right this second,' Azim Madam said. 'Is that right, little Mouth?'

Mouth nodded, not trusting herself to speak.

'Speak,' Azim Madam said with a slap. Her cheek stung.

'Yes 'ada', I could co' right this second,' Mouth said, feeling the indignity of her situation, wanting to stop speaking like an imbecile, or at least to close her lips so at least she wouldn't be drooling like one. And in the same moment she realized that Azim Madam had uncovered the core of her: an open mouth, craving, hungering, praying to be fucked. She had been lubricating for hours, she could taste the cum of every person in the room mingling together in her orifice, and the production of saliva and precum from her own glands was far, far beyond her own control. The truth was that nothing was in her control. Everything she was, every part of her sex, her self, was being controlled by the Madams. It was unbearable; she was the luckiest girl in the world.

And by the looks on their faces, the Madams knew it. Oh, they were very pleased with themselves; they would draw out this moment for their own satisfaction. The last resistance in Mouth melted away; she would give them everything they wanted, she would beg and plead and submit to their whims, their capriciousness and their cruelty.

''lease, 'ada's,' she said, trying to put all this into words, ''lease 'ay I co' for you?'

'We're not even touching her,' Azim Madam observed. In fact, they were: Nikhil's hand was on her neck, firmly controlling her movements, while Azim Madam had just begun idly fondling Mouth's nipples through the neosilk. She was trapped between them, but they were not touching her genitals at all. It didn't matter. She was so aroused that all she needed was permission.

'Nikki says you like pain,' Azim Madam mused, tossing her locks back and flicking a sharp blue fingernail at Mouth's now-erect nipple. 'Would you like a bit of pain with your orgasm, my precious Mouth?'

Oh, yes, please, anything just as long as you keep calling me yours, Mouth thought, since you own me already, every part of me.... Aloud she said, 'Yes 'lease, if it 'leases you, 'ada'.' Azim Madam smiled.

'When I pinch your nipple like this,' she said with a sudden, fierce twist that made Mouth cry out, 'you will come. Not before. You will come as many times as I choose, at the precise moments I choose. Do you understand?'

'Yes 'ada', I 'ill—' Mouth began, and was cut off by Azim Madam's lips covering hers. For a moment there was nothing else, no intrusion, no tongue-caresses: just this enclosure, this place of hot, erotic safety; this home.

The hard twist of her nipple surprised her, and she came as commanded, a small powerful orgasm flooding her mouth with her own cum, the taste as familiar to her as skin. Instinctively she tried to pull back, but Nikhil's grip was firm at the back of her neck. She had no choice but to submit to Azim Madam's rough exploration of her throbbing organ. Azim Madam lapped up Mouth's cum while making mmm-mmm sounds. *Devour me*, Mouth would have thought, if she'd been able to form words.

Then she started fucking Mouth, hard. The divided tongue, the dozens of neuro-crystals, all had Mouth ready for an orgasm again within mere seconds, and she tried to plead with moans and sounds. Her nipple twisted, and again the flood came. It happened over and over, without pause or rest in between convulsions, until Mouth felt lightheaded, losing all track of time, all count, all knowledge of her name or where she was; she was only this mouth, being so thoroughly ravaged, and this nipple that—ow! aaahhh—surely was about to be ripped off entirely, it hurt so much. A few times she felt Azim Madam's cum flow into her too, and she swallowed ecstatically, savouring the warm ambrosia all the way down her throat. Azim Madam left no part of her orifice unexplored; each of Mouth's precious neuro-crystals was given its own orgasm. The Madam bit lightly at the crystal at the tip of Mouth's tongue, then sucked on it, scraping her own labial neuro-crystals against it, hurting it more than Mouth would have thought possible, until the biting started again, when the previous layer of pain became just a dream. Pain and pleasure escalated each other, and her nipple was abused harshly again and again. Mouth came, and came, and came until she blacked out.

From a deep, floating dream of snakes and red clouds, Mouth awoke to Azim Madam's organ inside her again, fucking her awake. Mouth kissed her back passionately, trying to open her throat and suck the Madam off at the same time, and was rewarded by Azim Madam's sweet, spicy spurting. A twist of her sore nipple, and Mouth came too, wide awake and aware of how raw she felt.

'Good morning, sleepyhead,' Azim Madam said. 'Everyone else is already up.'

'Good 'orning, 'ada',' Mouth said shyly, memories of the wild evening flooding back in a rush, making her flush.

'Speak properly now,' Azim Madam said, a little briskly. 'That's going to get annoying soon. And you don't have to call me Madam anymore.'

Crushed, Mouth felt hot tears spring to her eyes, and she bit down on her lip to keep from crying, focusing on the cold harsh pain. Of course, she was just a plaything to Madam—to Azim. It was stupid to expect an orgy to end in ... well. Anything.

Mouth felt extremely, profoundly, humiliatingly stupid, and furiously sat up, looking around for her clothes. The jumpsuit was hanging on the bedframe, and she started pulling on the difficult outfit, which now felt humiliating rather than sexy.

Azim Madam remained seated on the edge of the bed. Mouth wished the woman, who suddenly seemed like a stranger again, would go away and let her have her come-down in privacy. Instead, Azim Madam watched her intently. Dressed, Mouth felt more naked than she could bear.

'Mouth,' Azim Madam said.

'My name is Leena,' Mouth said, but it sounded like a lie.

'Mouth,' Azim Madam insisted. 'Look at me.'

Mouth forced herself to meet the other woman's gaze, though she had to look away almost immediately.

'I think you've misunderstood me,' Azim Madam said. 'I meant that you don't have to call me Madam anymore, if you don't want to. The obligation connected to the party is over. If you do want to—well, I would be very flattered. You are—'

She paused, lowering her voice.

'As a Madam of the party, it was my responsibility to spread my attention around, and everyone here contributed to a wonderful evening. But you: you are simply the most amazing woman I have ever had the honour to meet.'

Mouth was speechless.

'And to fuck, of course,' Azim Madam said, smiling, so Mouth smiled too. Her whole body was tingling now, from her teeth to her toes, not with arousal but with something even more profound: joy.

'And,' the Madam continued, 'I think *love* is a very strong word. So I'd like you to know me a bit better before you decide if you want to say it again. Is that okay?'

Mouth nodded. *Of course. Anything you say is okay.* A tear began its slow, saline roll down the side of her nose.

'Do you have anywhere you have to be today?' Azim Madam asked.

Mouth shook her head. She could not have said what date it was, or perhaps even what month, but she knew she had left the day clear so that she could recover and enjoy the after-buzz of the party.

'Would you like to come home with me?'

Mouth nodded. There was nothing she could imagine wanting more.

The teardrop trembled at the corner of her lip.

'May I touch you?' Azim Madam asked.

Mouth almost laughed aloud. After giving so much, it was such a simple request—but they were, after all, at a beginning.

She assented. Azim reached out and, with one finger, wiped away the tear. Then she touched the fingertip to her tongue, savouring its salt.

'You are even more yummy than you looked,' she said, smiling.

'Thank you, Madam,' Mouth said, finally finding her voice. And then, boldly: 'So are you.'

Azim laughed out loud.

Mouth caught a spark in the Madam's eye—one of her own lip-crystals, reflected back. And she laughed too, letting all her questions and worries rest. There was so much to say, and at the same time nothing that needed to be said at all; and they had all day, maybe even forever, to say it.

A FOREIGNER

Amitava Kumar

They know I'm a foreigner. It makes me a little uneasy.
~ James Salter, A Sport and a Pastime

You are an immigrant. You turn on the radio one day and hear a woman's voice, a voice that is marked by a foreign accent, except the surprise is that she is talking about sex. She sounds like Henry Kissinger. Her name is Dr Ruth. Unlike Kissinger, she is about making love, not war. You listen to her on the small black radio in the privacy of your room. She offers advice to her male listeners. Even if they themselves have already climaxed, they can help their female partners achieve orgasm.

–You can just pleasure her.

You who speak in accented English haven't heard that verb before; you take note of the language and of the lesson that it drags behind it, a shimmering tail of light that trails a pale translucent body that will harden, become succulent, when warmed in a pan.

–And for women out there, a man wants an orgasm. Big deal! Give him an orgasm, it takes two minutes!

What a relief! For at least two reasons!

You discover details about her later. Dr Ruth grew up in an orphanage. Her parents perished at Auschwitz. She is very short but she fought in a war. She was a guerrilla in the Haganah. But in this country she is famous on radio, talking about masturbation and penises and vaginas. An extraordinary and busy life. She has been married thrice. *Dr Ruth, Dr Ruth, what is your favourite position.*

It was early March in Delhi, three days of spring. The year that I left India. We were in my room in the college dorm. An hour earlier, the daughter of the warden had walked past our window on her way to work, her hair still hanging damp on her lemon dupatta. We had quickly run to the end of the corridor to watch her open the little wooden gate on her way to the bus-stop. Upon our return, the conversation in the room had meandered with desultory charm.

–There is nothing purer than the love for your landlord's daughter, said Bheem.

–No, said Santosh, after an appropriate pause. If you are looking for innocence, the purest gangajal, you have to be in love with your teacher's wife.

As if to sort out the matter, we looked at Noni.

Noni, a Sikh from Patiala, took off his turban and his hair fell over his shoulders.

–You bastards should just stop pretending. The only true love, true first love, is the love for your maid-servant.

This was duly appreciated. But Noni was not done yet.

–She has to be older than you, though not by too much, and while it's not necessary for you to have fucked her, it is important that she take your hand in hers and put it on her breast.

There was the usual silence that greets the utterance of grand truth. Then, someone started laughing.

–You are a bunch of pussies, Noni said to dismiss the laughing. When you went back home during the winter, did any one of you get laid?

He smiled and announced his own success with a question.

–Has anyone slept with a friend's mother?

–I have, Bheem said. He was smiling a soft, secret smile.

–Whose mother, Noni asked.

–Yours.

After I met Nina, I would buy magazines like *Cosmopolitan* from the supermarket if it had headlines like 'Ten Hottest Things You Can Say In Bed' or 'Seventy Seven Sex Positions'. What did I learn from them? That I was supposed to say Is it okay with you if I take this slow? I also bought *Romance for Dummies*. Dr Ruth encouraged you to make noise while having sex. She wrote: While you retain the right to remain silent, perhaps you could speak up a little before your final act.

Even a four-letter word. She said you never know how you'll react unless you give it a try at least one time. I enacted a silly pantomime when I came inside Nina that first time, not a war whoop exactly, more of a raised fist celebrating the revolutionary storming of the barricades, but noticed that she was silent, even pensive, though later that night she was affectionate, smiling, and this took away some of my foreboding.

I am telling you this in Immigration Court, Your Honour, because I want to assert that I knew about sex, I spoke about sex, I discoursed about sex, prior to my arrival on these shores. I have chosen to speak in personal terms, the most intimate terms, Your Honour, because it seems to me that it is this crucial part of humanity that is denied to the immigrant. You look at a dark immigrant in that long line in JFK, the new clothes crumpled from the long flight, a ripe smell accompanying him, his eyes haunted, and you wonder whether he can speak English. It is far from your thoughts and your assumptions to ask whether he has ever spoken soft phrases filled with yearning or, who knows, what dirty words he utters in his wife's ear as she laughs and touches him in bed. You look at him and think that he wants your job but not that he just wants to get laid. I thank you in the name of the dark hordes that have nothing to declare but their desire.

I had enrolled in a film seminar. Nina was also in it. She had short-cropped hair, large brown eyes and full lips. Her movements were full of allure. Even when she was not moving, just sitting in the dark watching the films that were screened for us, I was always aware of the outline of her face. Sometimes, instead of the film, I'd watch the light fluctuating on her face. One day, during an intermission of Sidney Lumet's *Dog Day Afternoon*, I saw her at the water fountain. She raised her face, her mouth still wet.

–I wanted to ask you something, I said to her.

–You want to know whether I'm fertile?

She laughed and looked at me.

I laughed too but for a moment I didn't know what to say.

–Is it possible that you are ovulating? What came out instead was: Are you going to be in Comp Lit 300?

–As a matter of fact, I am! How can I not enrol in a course that appears on the transcript as CLIT 300?

The following week, in the film class, we were discussing Nagisa Oshima's *In the Realm of the Senses*. The professor, a small Frenchwoman whose face and neck would get covered in hives if you asked uncomfortable questions, had put the film on pause. An Italian girl was engaged in a long discussion with her about Japanese cinema; she had recently watched a film about a nuclear explosion on Mt Fuji. Nina was sitting in the chair next to me. I don't know what possessed me but I passed a scrap of paper to her. On it I had written:

Wet moss between your thighs

Semen

Rains on Mount Fuji

She surprised me by putting out a small tongue out as if she was licking ice cream.

The next semester we were together in CLIT 300, 'Brecht and His Friends'. We saw each other twice a week; I flirted with her more confidently because I saw that she didn't take me seriously. Once in class, I stepped in and saw that Nina was seated in a circle of four or five others. I noticed right away that her outfit, a pale raw silk vest over a sleeveless cotton shirt, had been made in India. Those clothes could have been from Bloomingdale's but as far as I was concerned they might well have been a gift from me. I stepped close behind her and felt the fabric of her vest with my fingertips.

–Nice. I see that my cousin did a good job on his wooden weaving machine. He had been having trouble in his garden with the silk-spinning caterpillars.

I didn't check to see if the others were amused or full of contempt. Probably both. All that mattered was that Nina was smiling.

–Your cousin? Was it the one who lost his arm in the war?

I had no idea what she was talking about.

–The very same, madam. Just last month he was brought to London to present a bolt of the finest cloth to the Queen for the Festival of India. Thank you for having ruled over us.

–Well, you must thank your cousin when you next see him. Tell him the mills of northern England say sorry for having stolen his business.

Your Honour, by the standards of a court of law, we were full of lies. But how liberating were those lies! They gave me so much pleasure! Whereas the truthfulness of the others would have banished me to the Siberia of Silence, Nina warmly welcomed me with those lies to the warm and joyful America of invention.

I laughed at her remark. I didn't want the banter to end.

–The mills are now all closed, and I hear they are all full of regret.

–Yes, serve the fuckers right.

She was sitting down and I couldn't clap her back, so I laughed and put my palm on the back of her neck. She immediately lowered her head, as if I had just announced that I was going to give her a massage. And that is what I proceeded to do, slowly make circles at the base of her skull with my thumbs, my eyes fixed on the point where her hair was the shortest. I was conscious that all talk in the room had ceased but I wasn't going to stop. With my fingers lightly gripping Nina's shoulders, I rubbed my thumbs on the small bones of her bare neck. Her skin felt cool and I was flooded with a sense of peace.

This was the first time I had touched Nina. I hid my erection by pressing against the back of the chair. I tried to breathe normally. I stayed quiet although the silence seemed to weigh the moment with a significance I didn't dare recognize. I began to blabber.

–Madam, I come from a long line of mystic masseurs.

–Evidently.

The professor, David Lamb, walked in. Quiet, precise, wearing glasses that, a decade later, would be called Franzensque. Lamb noticed what I was doing but didn't remark on it. I bet he would have liked to get into bed with Nina. It would no doubt happen very naturally with him. They would sit at one of the restaurants uptown, drinking wine with cheese and olives, exchanging jokes about a performance they had both seen separately at the Papp Theater. One of them would mention dinner, and the other would readily agree. When night came, it would only simplify rather than complicate things. And in the morning, Lamb would pick up his stylish glasses from the side table and look at her smiling at him. When she sat up, he'd say something funny and she would bend down and kiss him on that impressive nose.

I removed my hands from the back of Nina's neck and took the last remaining seat that was across from her. If Nina was at all conscious that we had been engaged in an intimate act she didn't reveal it. Our eyes didn't meet during the rest of the class.

The dirty snow that had stayed stuck seemingly for months under the dumpster and around the electric pole finally melted. It was April and while looking at a bench in the park it struck me that I could now sit outside without the frigid air making my penis shrink and vanish inside my stomach. And there were daffodils! Show me an immigrant from India or Jamaica or Kenya who isn't thrilled to see the first daffodils of spring. The honest person forced to memorize Wordsworth's 'Daffodils' without having a clue about what those flowers looked like can celebrate the fact that he isn't any longer in the dark. We now know what those flowers look like. We have arrived!

I had just had lunch and was on my way to the library. I told myself that I could read later, when darkness had fallen, and that right now, I should perhaps find a friend to have a beer with. Peter was probably in the TA room, slaving over Horkheimer. He could be easily persuaded to put on his stolen Ray Bans and sit outside in the sun at Salty Dog.

The lights were off in the TA room, but Nina was there, sitting at her desk, her face bathed in white under her table lamp. A green frog jumped out of my chest and plopped down in the little pool of light beneath Nina's chin.

–Comrade Nina!

In response, an amused shake of the head. *Hiya*. A balanced mix of enthusiasm and indifference.

–Comrade IRS to you, my friend. I'm trying to do my taxes.

With a dramatic flourish I extracted from my backpack a yellow folder I had been carrying for a week: my W-2 statement, a dozen receipts from the University bookstore, the flight and hotel receipts from the graduate student conference on Salman Rushdie in Atlanta.

–Nina, I beg you. Please stop. Let's do our taxes together.

–Why would I want to do anything so painful with you?

–Comrade IRS, let's have a beer. But let's also do our taxes together. I cannot make head or tail of those forms.

She agreed that it was glorious outside, gathered her papers and switched off her lamp.

Your Honour, as you are well aware, that is what the Statue of Liberty says. Give me your tired, your poor, huddled masses, and I will help them file their taxes.

Our TA office was in the shadow of the tall science building, the light that filtered in through the window weak, half-nocturnal. For a moment, she stood still, thinking. A fish suspended in water. A thin blue sweater hung loosely from her shoulders. Something clicked in her mind, and she darted toward the door, all brisk efficiency.

–Do you have the forms?

–No!

On the way to her hatchback, we stopped at the campus post-office to pick up the forms. Every chair at Salty Dog accommodated a loud frat boy, so Nina grabbed a blanket and cooler from her apartment and we went to the botanical garden instead. It had a hill that rose up till you came to a small stone tower built to commemorate the death of sailors at sea. Was it on that first visit, or later, that she told me that all those vessels that had gone down were slave ships? No mention on the plaque of the hundreds cramped together under the grated hatchways, men and women and small children drowned with the manacles still bound around their legs and necks.

We laid out the blanket on the grass. In the cooler I found five bottles of beer and, in a silver foil bag, spoons and a tub of ice cream. In the distance, maybe five hundred yards away, visible through the black trees that were still bare, was a road on which a car occasionally passed. Otherwise, in the middle of this workday afternoon, we could have been on another planet. Nina laid herself down on her stomach, pen in hand, the pages of Form 1040NR spread out in front of her. *Name and address*, she said, and without waiting for me to reply, began to write.

Filing Status

Exemptions

Adjusted Gross Income

Line of Your Spine
Oh, Nina's Legs
Ass-Stupa

I readily responded to her questions, mostly by making up my answers, and like a shrewd lawyer she accepted what I told her. Only once she warned, *Don't fuck with the State. I don't want to see you deported.* Did she mean it in the way I hoped? Later, she would say yes, but, in this and other instances, I keep an open mind. *The only point worth considering here, Your Honour, is that it was the solemn enactment of the fundamental duty of the citizen, paying taxes, which brought us together.* While she showed her agility with numbers, I smelled the grass and imagined smelling her, imagined pulling her skirt down the length of her smooth legs. Her breasts were pressed against the hard ground. I wanted to cup them, hold them gently, patiently, while she quickly multiplied one thousand ninety-four point one nine by six.

She brought her calculations to a close. It turned out that $187 was to be refunded to me. I signed my name at the bottom of the form. *Thank you*, I said, *thank you.*

She pushed her shades up on her head.

–What are you going to do with your dollars?

–Can I take you out for dinner?

I took her for dinner to La Cucaracha. With the first sip of my drink, a fine calmness descended on me. I wasn't acting cocky and, to be honest, my mind wasn't entirely free of doubt. Still, I wasn't worried about Nina and me anymore. There was no anxiety. In fact, there were moments when I felt certain that this woman who was laughing and mocking me as she ate corn tortilla chips was waiting for me to kiss her.

–You are in some terrible situation on a ship, let's say, Nina said. A field trip gone horribly wrong. And the only way you can escape is if you slept with one of your professors. The question is: who would you *not* sleep with, like never, never, not in a million years to save your fucking life?

–Bonnie Clark.

–That was too easy. Let me change the question: who would you absolutely want to sleep with, even if you were doing this only because the pirates who had captured you were going to kill you otherwise?

–I would sleep with you. Instead, I said, I'm not afraid of death.

–Why can't a dog tell a lie? Is it because he is too honest, or is it because he is too sly? Poor Wittgenstein!

I had not read Wittgenstein. But David Lamb had read Wittgenstein, and Hegel, and Kant, and Stanley Cavell. Lamb had once said at a party that whenever he suffered from insomnia he read Derrida. *Not because he makes me go to sleep but because he makes staying up a pleasure.* As I thought of Lamb, a sliver of ice lodged itself in my heart. My earlier assurance ebbed, and I felt stranded on the shore, watching the boat slowly receding. Our dinner of skirt steak and jumbo shrimp was nearly over, and now because I was uncertain why we had been laughing only a minute ago, a sense of fatalism began to overtake me. The fickle human heart, prone to despair. How quickly the boredom sets in.

Perhaps Nina noticed a change.

–Okay, truth-teller, she said, it is time to get you off this ship and into your bed.

I was relieved when I saw that Nina didn't turn onto her street, that she was going to drive me back to my place first. Now that I saw that I wasn't going to be asked if I wanted to come to her apartment, I could relax again. I thought I'd really like to find a cigarette.

–I said cheerfully, You know what I'd like right now?

–A blow job?

I laughed, and she laughed too.

When she dropped me off, Nina said she needed to use the bathroom. I heard the noise of the flush in the toilet and, as soon as she came out in the hallway, I said to her in a sudden rush, Don't leave.

My hand went up to her cheek.

Finally. She made those quotations marks in the air with two fingers of both hands when she said that word.

A person who is laughing is difficult to kiss, so I hesitated a moment. She put a finger on my mouth and leaned in closer, a serious expression on her face. The soft crush of her mouth on mine released a fury of desire in me. We kissed for a long time, standing in that hallway, Nina pressed firmly against the wall.

I am from a land of famines, Your Honour, and I displayed such hunger, such astonishing greed. I was hungry for her lips, her tongue, the small whorl in her ear, even her hair. Eager to touch every part of her, I turned Nina around so that her back was to me. She raised her arms, her palms flat against the wall. I was the blind man, feeling the different parts of her body. I took her breasts in my hands. One afternoon in Delhi, Noni had gone with Deepali from Sociology to Surajkund. They came back late. What did he most like about her? Noni said that Deepali's breasts were like kabootars in his hands, two soft, startled pigeons fluttering under his fingers. This is the truth of my American Dream: to possess the life of a Sikh from Patiala. At least, that is what the dream was till I met Nina and she took me, almost daily, to other neighbourhoods. In my teens, I had made many guilty entries in my journal. I never once wrote down the word 'masturbation'; I only recorded that I was 'distracted'. In my teens, I had been innocent of something as mundane as a Victoria's Secret catalogue. Your Honour, Nina made such self-consciousness a thing of the past. Nina, once we became lovers, rid me of my guilt. She'd examine the pictures in the catalogue and ask me which model I wanted to fuck. Where do you want to do it, the wooden deck visible toward the top of the picture, or right here on the sandy beach where she has planted her red toenails? Smoothly wrapping her fingers around my cock, a supple breast against me, her breath hot on my ear, she would command me to demonstrate how I'd have my way with the freckled model after I had ripped off those new black and white panties from her ass. I'm aware, Your Honour, of the language I'm using but may I proceed to the bench to present evidence? This is Nina in an email dated 29 April, 1996: 'You'll have to slap me with the hand that's on my hip, the other has my clit in a soft pinch, you're rubbing it between your fingers, and when you hit me, when your cock twitches inside me, it shivers, and some new wave of wetness washes down between my thighs.'

All through that afternoon, while she had helped me with my taxes, I had coveted Nina's legs criss-crossed on the woollen blanket. Now, I was crouching down in the hallway, beside my bike that I had bought from a Chinese electrical engineering student for twenty bucks, and kissing the back of her knees. I kissed her and licked her, pushing my tongue everywhere I could. In touching her legs I was touching the sea, I was walking on soft sand, I was tasting the salt of the limitless water. I heard her sigh when I moved my hands up to her crotch. I pulled down her panties with my teeth. Nina said, Let's go to your bed.

I apologize, Your Honour, but even at that moment, I could almost hear my mind repeating clichés, Such a long journey. Not from hallway to bed, but from the long wanting to the moment of fulfilment. That is what sex with Nina had meant to me: keen desire and struggle, and, just when it seemed that the goal was still so far, success. This ache that I had nursed so long, as if for a lifetime, ended with Nina naked under me. A pair of white thighs opening, legs wrapped around my torso and then spread wide. Her head was inching closer to the wall behind her, and putting my hand protectively on her hair, I moved deeper into her. Her moans soon turned, with a half-gasp, into the phrase that the article in *Cosmopolitan* had said every man wants to hear, I'm going to come. *Hallelujah. There is no God but God, and I can't quite remember his name. You are my station, my docking port, my floating runway lit with a million lights. You are my home away from home. From now on, I will speak the truth, the whole truth, and nothing but the truth. My darling, I love you, now and forever.*

SEMEN, SALIVA, SWEAT, BLOOD

Hansda Sowvendra Shekhar

NIRMAL

'Saali,' Nirmal Mahato says, laying his entire weight on my back, 'chhilti kaahe nahi hai be gaand ka baal ko? Mera lund mein lagta hai.' Bitch, why don't you shave the hair in your arse? It hurts my dick.

'Aap jo humko itna chodte hain daaru peeke,' I reply, smarting, 'humko nahi lagta hai kya?' And when you fuck me like this, drunk, don't you think I'm hurt as well?

He draws his penis out of my sore asshole and slaps my buttocks. 'Toh chudti kaahe hai, saali?' So why do you want to be fucked, bitch?

'Achchha lagta hai, jaan.' I feel good, love. I smile at him, relieved that he has lifted his weight off me.

'Sudhregi nahin, madarchod.' You'll not change, motherfucker.

He slumps beside me, his arousal waning. I have to suck him again. For a man, getting an erection when he's drunk is difficult. Unless he's going to fuck a woman, with boobs and a cunt. This is what Nirmal has told me.

Yet, I like him drunk. Because when he's drunk, he doesn't care that I'm not a woman. I only have to arouse him, either by massaging his gym-toned shoulders or sucking his penis. I'm the first man he's ever screwed. I saw it in his intoxicated eyes when I first gave him a blow job—the surprise, the hesitation, and the escape. When he returned for more, I knew I had to keep him, whatever it took. Men are hard to find, and here was one with a body to die for fucking me.

I licked his broad, sweat-soaked chest with its day-old crop. I licked his tits.

'Madarchod,' he grunts. I am doing a great job.

I lick his abs, stick my tongue in his navel. He jumps up. I giggle. He hates being touched there.

'Sudhrega nahin, laura ka baal!' You won't change, you asshole!

This—his addressing me as a male—was, certainly, not a compliment. 'Sorry.' I go straight to where I should've reached earlier and pull down his foreskin, with its tiny mole on the right side. His glans smells of alcohol, my own anus, and our lube, Johnson's Baby Oil. I lick his whole penis, very gently, stroking the perineum at the same time.

'Maa-dar-chood.'

This is a compliment. I continue. Lick, slurp, stroke, ah-ah. Ah–lick–ah–slurp–ah–slurp–ah–lick ...

He holds my head still. 'Lie down. Lie on your stomach.'

The condoms are finished. He takes the baby oil and puts some on his penis, gives it to me so that I can lube myself. He folds my left leg at the knee and pins my right leg straight. He's so strong, this man who lifts and pumps iron, that I can't move even an inch.

He starts fucking me.

'Aaahh ...' Pain? Pleasure? I don't know for sure. All I know is that I long to be fucked by Nirmal, my precious man.

'Chupp!' Shut up! He places a hand over my mouth. His penis slides in and out of my anus, hurting, stimulating the inside of my perineum. 'Saali, next time I want it shaved,' he commands, pumping, drilling wildly, stimulating my prostate, squeezing my chest with both his hands. I feel like I might bleed and ejaculate at the same time.

'Ah! Ah!' he groans. He's about to come. I move my buttocks upwards to counter his thrusts, turning my head to look at his expression. He lets out a smile, that intoxicated smile I love to see. 'Come on, come on,' he whispers.

He ejaculates and slumps over me. We remain motionless for about a minute, my powerful man lying in a powerless heap on top of me. His naked skin against mine, in an embrace that I wish could last forever. He rises. I hold his arm.

'Don't go,' I plead. 'Lie down with me for a few more seconds.' I want to keep him with me forever so we can fuck every hour of the day, every minute. But that will never happen. All I can do is keep him with me for as long as possible.

He wipes his penis with an old newspaper, drinks a litre of water in a gulp, gets dressed and sprawls in a chair in front of me. I watch him, hold out my hand.

He doesn't take it. Sex over, senses restored.

'Too much hard work, boss,' he says. His calling me 'boss'—the traditional way in which a junior addresses his senior—gives me a chill. *What am I doing? Fucking with a junior?* I'm twenty-seven, one year older than him, already doing my housemanship while he has yet to clear his degree exam. Also, he is a Mahato, from a different 'phylum'. I am an Adivasi, and not enough that I had an 'intimate' Mahato friend, I was also letting him screw me. A spark of shame races through me. He may be the top in sex, but I was the one who started this relationship, drew him to me. An Adivasi being fucked—quite literally—by a Kurmi, and the stupid Adivasi enjoying it.

'Please, wash yourself.' He covers my naked body with my chadar, the brute in him gone.

'Don't go,' I plead.

'I have to,' he asserts.

'Why are you being so gentle now? You're so rough when we are doing that.'

'When we do it again, I'll be rough.'

'When?'

'Next time.'

'Now.'

'No.'

'Why?'

'I have to go.'

I throw the chadar off and he jumps from the chair and out of the door, shutting it behind him so that no one else sees me naked. When I'm sure he's not returning I wrap a gumchha around me and head to the bathroom.

I want to touch his semen. From the hairy mesh of my anus I extricate something sticky. It could either be his semen or my shit. I hold it near my nostrils. It smells of both, and also of Johnson's Baby Oil. I get a hard on. I run my hands over my body, over my breasts which are still smarting from his squeezing. I pinch my nipples hard, like he does. I grip my penis and start to jerk off. I see both of us sweaty and pumping. I smell his sweat, alcohol and cigarettes. Maa-daar-chood. I ejaculate into my hand.

They called Nirmal the Salman Khan of our medical college. He had built his body like him, walked, talked and danced like him, and, in the last few years, had even started drinking like him. The juniors idolized him, posing for photographs with him, their shirts off, flexing their biceps. These photos got enthusiastic comments on Facebook: 'The real dabangg', 'Nirmal boss ka jalwa', 'No one can have a better body than Nirmal boss'. He was starting to get a paunch from the drinking but his chest and biceps were still hard as rock.

The front licence plate of his bike—a huge, blue Pulsar 200—read YUVRAAJ, after the film starring Salman Khan. Except, the film's title had an extra V. I told him he should fix it.

He thought about it. 'I need some money.'

'How much?'

'I think ... five hundred would do.'

Even as I handed him the note, I knew he wouldn't fix it. I knew I was doing this to keep him. I had no other way, because I needed a man, someone as special as Sunit.

Sunit

Sunit Besra was the intellectual, the athlete, the aesthete, the ambitious one. He was my classmate, just two months and three weeks older than me. He was from the same 'phylum'. Adivasi; a Santhal, like me; and though he put up 'Agnostic' as his religion on his Orkut profile, his family was—like mine—Sarna. He played badminton and football; loved photography and junk food; read Osho; watched BBC; had 'Veni Vidi Vici' printed on the front licence plate of his red Pulsar 150; made me read Tagore's stories to him because he loved my accent. A junior once told us we looked like brothers. We went to book fairs and bonded over Rabindranath-Ray-Rituparno. He wanted me to teach him Santhali. Before his football match, he'd ask me to keep his glasses because, he reasoned, 'I trust you.'

'Why aren't you a girl?' he joked with me. 'I'd have married you.'

We had been good friends for a little over two years when we became lovers. It all started the afternoon he showed me his dick. He was changing, but instead of putting on his jeans he opened the towel and gave me a fleeting glimpse of his penis. Then he rewrapped the towel around him, wore the jeans, winked, and then kissed me. His lips were like juicy orange slices. He played with my tongue, inserting his into my mouth, our teeth colliding. I guided his hands to my breasts and he squeezed them. I asked him to suck my tits, to bite them, to hurt me. He licked them first, *lap lap lap lap*, like a pussycat finishing a bowl of milk; then he bit them, like a dog on a bone. And when I had squealed enough, he directed my hand to his penis, hard and straight like a flashlight.

'Give me a BJ,' he demanded.

Sunit's penis was like a porn star's, his shiny glans emerging from the foreskin like a pearl from an oyster. When I took his penis in my mouth he sighed and combed his Dhoni-like, nape-length hair back with his fingers.

'Should I?' he asked before ejaculating.

'Hmm ...' I signalled with my right hand that he could ejaculate into my mouth. He tasted soapy. Semen always tastes soapy, whoever the man.

Spent, he lay curled into himself.

'I'm sorry,' he said to me, head turned to the other side, not facing me. *Sorry for what?*

'That's okay,' I said, inching closer to him, touching his back. He shrugged me away.

'Go,' he said.

'I wanted to—'

'No,' he said, louder, his head still turned to the other side. 'Before someone sees us, leave. Please.'

I'd lent him my disc of Ray's *Aranyer Din Ratri*. The picnic game in the movie later became a method of foreplay.

'Sex,' he said.

'Sex, dick,' I responded.

'Sex, dick, semen.'

'Sex, dick, semen, erection.'

'Sex, dick, semen, erection, orgasm.'

That's as far as we got. Aroused, we undressed and got down to business. My chewing gum got entangled in his bush as I blew him hungrily.

He winced. 'Betichod, daant nahin!' Daughterfucker, no teeth!

Once we started fucking, our friendship was replaced by arousals, erections and orgasms. Sunit couldn't acknowledge me anymore. From the day we became lovers, our discussions on literature and art house cinema stopped. He made sure we were not seen together in public. I didn't really care. I wanted this more than the friendship.

Whenever he needed me he gave me a call. A missed call, usually. At four in the morning, after he'd finished his reasoning and data interpretation exercises, when nearly everyone in the hostel was asleep.

Sakula sisigela. 'Childhood', from the *Mandela* soundtrack, was my ringtone at that time. Four a.m. My heartbeat raced as I peered at the display. Sunit.

If I took his call, the conversation would be just two-words long.

'Come,' he'd say.

'Yes,' I'd answer.

Disconnect.

I would put Johnson's Baby Oil on the parts he'd soon touch, spray deodorant over my carotids, chew two Orbit gums and, making sure there was no one in the corridors, pass stealthily by the rooms of doctors staying up late studying for PG entrance exams until I reached his room on the second floor.

If we hadn't started fucking, we'd have stayed good friends. We'd still discuss Rituparno Ghosh's films. I'd read him passages from my stories, from the books I purchased. We'd exchange DVDs, go to the film festival, raid roadside paav bhaaji stalls, talked to each other in fluent Santhali.

Just days before he left the hostel and the medical stream to become a capitalist businessman, after I went down on him and he'd ejaculated in my mouth, he told me blithely that he was planning to get married to a girl he'd chosen. She was a doctor, a beautiful Santhal woman with a broad, benignant smile.

'Please,' he begged, 'don't spoil my marriage.'

Lucky

After it ended with Sunit, another of our classmates, Lucky, became my lover. If there ever were fights with outsiders intruding on our college property, Sunit and Lucky were among the first ones to jump in. They'd grab the collars of the intruders, and without giving them a chance to explain, shower volleys of punches and kicks on the hapless men.

Lucky and I would go on bike rides and get drunk together. He had this habit of chewing Rajnigandha and Tulsi—paan masala and its gutkha adjuvant—something I found very uncouth and irritating.

'Why do you have to chew that?' I asked him.

'Have you seen a scooter being filled?' he asked back.

'Yes.'

'What do they do?'

'Well, they fill it up with petrol. Then they put Mobil into it.'

'Well, this Rajnigandha is my petrol and Tulsi is my Mobil. My fuel and lubricant.'

He was like a child, heavily into Nagraj, Dhruv and Doga comics and computer games. He didn't read my short stories but did help me pack my printed A4 sheets into large, unwieldy envelopes. He danced with hired dancers at our college festivals, flipping notes at those garishly dressed women gyrating to Bollywood item songs and crude Bhojpuri songs like 'Saiyaji dilwa maange la gumchha bichhai ke'—my man spreads a gumchha on the floor and asks for my heart. His ideal woman, however, was Amrita Rao's character in *Vivah*. He had a pencil sketch of hers pasted on a wall of his room. He always had several female friends at the same time, but only one special one to whom he couriered stuffed hearts and teddy bears. When that special friend came to town he arranged for a hotel room for the two of them.

Lucky had this streamlined, Cornetto-like body that tapered towards the bottom. Broad above, narrow below; chest thrown out; shoulders wide; bulky, muscular arms; straight back; and cute, taut, squeeze-worthy buns. He had a flabby paunch, used dumbbells, kept a baseball club under his bed. He called me 'gadrayil badan': succulent body.

Lucky and I had first had sex in his room. The night started out at a bar. Nirmal—slimmer in those days, a regular gym-goer seriously into bodybuilding, riding a simple Hero Honda Splendor, and seriously in love with a bitch of a female classmate of his—had come with us, though I barely knew him then. I touched Lucky's crotch with my toes from under the table and he spread his legs wide, nodding his head to the sensation I was causing. Nirmal—innocent-faced, wide-eyed—watched us in dazed amusement.

'What are you watching?' I growled at Nirmal.

'You are touching boss's dick,' he said, deadpan.

Lucky and I broke into laughter.

I went to Lucky's room after the bar. He took off his clothes and wrapped a towel around himself.

'Can I kiss you?' I asked.

'Sure,' he said.

We probed each other's mouths with our tongues.

'I want to fuck you,' he said.

I took my clothes off, got on all fours.

He slipped on a condom, and as Khaled's 'Didi' played from his CD player, I lubricated my hole with his Parachute Coconut Oil. Lucky's penis was like a carrot, small and straight. It entered my hole easily, like the pins of a plug going into a socket.

Didi, didi, didi, didi, zin di wah

Thrust thrust thrust ...

Didi wah, didi

'Ah ah ah ah ...'

Didi, didi, zin di wah

'It hurts? Does it hurt? Ah! Ah! Does it hurt?'

Didi wah, didi

'Noooh ... Noooh ... It's gooood, it's gooood, go on, go on ...'

Didi di hazzine daaayyeeeah

Lucky and I fucked a few more times after that, usually when we were drunk. We'd ride on his black Pulsar 150 to a dhaba outside the town for beer and rum. On the way back, I'd fondle his chest, quickly removing my hands on seeing the headlights of an approaching vehicle. We returned to either his room or mine and did it wherever we could. On the bed, on the floor, against the wall. It was exciting at first, but I soon grew tired of it. Sex with Sunit had a decorum to it, like a meeting of envoys. It was sanitised, with a pattern. Sex with Lucky was wild. Biting, scratching, hitting each other. Semen, saliva, sweat, blood. Though I loved wild sex I couldn't help noticing that we were doing it real dirty. And Lucky seemed to be doing it for alcohol.

'Daaru,' he'd demand, showing up at my room with only a towel wrapped around him.

If I refused, he forced his way in anyway—he knew I needed sex, that I'd let him seduce me. He took off his towel as if he were doing a Chippendale act, removed my shirt, sucked my tits till I begged to be fucked, then he fucked me and I paid for his drinks.

One night, however, I refused him anything and pushed him out of my room.

'Besra's gone, I'll go too. Let's see if you find someone better,' he sneered before he left, holding on to the towel tightly lest it slipped from his waist.

Nirmal

There's something about a man who pumps iron and has rippling muscles and four-pack abs. It is taken for granted that he fucks well. There were always people talking about Nirmal in the hostel corridors, about his female conquests—women who worked at gents' beauty parlours; horny, full-bodied, divorced bhabhijis who lived alone; nurses. Lucky had challenged me if I could find someone better and I decided it would be Nirmal—I'd show Lucky just how much better I'd done.

After not having talked with Nirmal for nearly a year—except those social niceties—one evening I invited him to my room. He wasn't the same Nirmal who'd seen me toeing Lucky's crotch. This Nirmal was a broken man. He'd failed to clear a few of his exams and had been made to repeat two years; his girlfriend had left him for a senior; he had stopped going to the gym and had grown a paunch, though his body was still worth dying for; and he was drinking heavily.

He plopped himself on a chair. 'Hi boss,' he said. 'Lucky boss talks about you all the time. Why don't you go and see him?' Lucky now worked in a different hospital in a different part of the town. Nirmal spent all his evenings drinking with Lucky in his flat.

I ignored his question. 'You tell me,' I asked mischievously, 'which girl are you seeing right now?'

He smiled coyly. 'She's a nurse in Lucky boss's hospital.'

'How did you do it?'

'In the missionary position. Me on top.'

Top? Ah! I could imagine.

A few days later, I invited him out for drinks. We were both high on cocktails of vodka and rum when we returned to my room. I hugged him, said, 'I want to kiss you,' my palms sweaty at propositioning a junior. A guy junior.

'What?' he asked, surprised.

I didn't speak, just stuck my lips to his and sucked hard.

He sucked back, and when we were done, I told him, my heart beating hard at each word, 'Tera lund choosna hai.' I want to suck your dick.

'What?' This time he smiled, incredulous, forcing his droopy, intoxicated eyes to look up at me.

I started to pull down his fly.

'Wait, wait,' he unzipped his jeans. He wasn't wearing underwear. His penis was hard. Success. I pushed the foreskin back and licked the glans.

'Ah!' he sighed.

But when I put it all in my mouth and started sucking it, he drew it out.

'No, no, boss,' he said. 'Not right, we are both men.'

'Fuck me, then.' My Plan B. I slid out of my trousers and underwear and bent before him. 'Come.'

He thrust his penis into my anus. No aim, no inclination, no lubricant. I screamed. Frightened, he put on his jeans and ran away, only to return a few minutes later.

'My bike's run out of petrol.'

I gave him a hundred.

That evening, Lucky called me. Nirmal must have told him.

'Child abuse, eh?' he asked.

'No,' I said, without a hint of shame or contrition. 'Consenting adults.'

To my surprise, Nirmal came to me the next morning. I woke up and there he was, sober and ready.

I bent on all fours, lifted my buttocks up at him in the sexiest way I knew, and put a handful of Johnson's Baby Oil into my anus.

'Badhiya chuttad hai.' You have a nice ass, he said, stroking my buttocks. 'You know, boss, we couldn't do it yesterday because you hadn't lubricated it. Lubrication is very necessary.'

He undressed and slipped on a condom. He looked like a man out of those protein supplement ads, with pumped up chests and biceps. Bending down on all fours, I spread my legs.

'Lie down,' he said, touching my buttocks and back.

What? Lie down? I was used to being fucked doggy-style. That way I too had the liberty of movement, the convenience of doing my backing and fronting. Lie down? With this giant on top of me? I'd be crushed.

'Lie down.' He was already on top of me, his penis on my back, his lips on my nape, kissing me.

'It's better—'

'Shut up and lie down,' he put his weight over me and pinned me down. 'There's no time.'

No one had ever used force with me. Not Lucky, and certainly not Sunit. But Nirmal did it and I liked it. I let him flex my left knee and climb on top of me, but I wasn't prepared for what was coming.

Sunit's penis was like a porn star's, Lucky's was a carrot, but Nirmal's penis was perfect. The right kind. Black like his body, thick like his arms, substantial but not intimidating. Yet, when it began probing me, despite all that lubricant, I felt like I'd die that very moment.

'Shh ... It hurts? It won't,' he lulled me, kissed my cheek, my nape, and pumped again. And again. And again and again and again and again. And all the while I waited for the ordeal to end.

'Gira dein aapke andar?' he asked chivalrously. Should I ejaculate inside you?

'Yes,' I mumbled. I appreciated his asking this, though it did not matter where he ejaculated as he was wearing a condom.

That day I gave him two hundred.

Nirmal was magical. For a while, at least, he made me forget Sunit. I returned to the hostel from work, smelly from delivering babies in the labour room and the OT, and instead of taking a shower and changing into clean clothes I went to his room on the second floor and sucked his dick, marvelling at how similar cunt and dick smelt. On other occasions he would pick me up from work and we went out to drink. We came back late at night and slept in my room on the ground floor, fucking before sleeping, fucking after getting up in the morning. I wondered about the other women in his life but kept quiet about it. I was his first and only Facebook friend, but when, after a few months, spurred by a newfound confidence at having cleared his exams, he started adding more friends, the thought of sharing him made me so jealous I unfriended him. He had no idea till I told him, and he seemed unfazed. Facebook wasn't that important to him, nor was my friendship.

'I'll never leave you, jaanu,' he said, taking my confused, uncertain body in his arms and kissing my cheeks.

He had a serious girlfriend now. He called her 'Moti', roly-poly. I imagined her to be homely and cute; not a slut like me, or the ones he'd screwed. That's how he talked to her, mollycoddling her as if she were a baby, turning from rogue to gentleman, chivalrously helping her with her array of problems: a missed bus, a taxing training programme, indigestion.

I knew he'd never tell me her real name. All I knew—mostly from spying—was that she lived in Santhal Pargana, a night's journey from our town; she worked in a bank; and—like me—she found his snoring annoying. I consoled myself with the thought that while Moti was waiting for her Nirmal, I was the one having sex with him.

Nirmal was all over me, on my body, inside my head. I tried to keep it physical but he captured my mind. Shamelessly, he called me whenever he needed me, even when I was at work. He came drunk and banged and spat at my door or bellowed my name loud in his sexy, bull-like voice for the entire floor to hear. Secretly, I loved it.

I couldn't concentrate on anything, was afraid I'd end up neglecting my patients. He lied to me, made up stories about himself and the women he'd had. He told me he also dealt in arms, that he knew the area commanders of Communist rebels and coal mafias of Dhanbad, that the scar he had on his shoulder was where a goonda had touched him with a burning cigarette, and that he had punched that goonda to a pulp. Later on, he told me that the scar was self-inflicted, because he wanted to have a scar like Salman Khan had. With each story I desired him more. With each story, I gave in further to his brutish mystique. To absolve myself of any guilt stemming out of fucking with a junior, I laid down three conditions:

1. *That he'd treat me like an equal or even an inferior (complete with expletives and violence), if not in public then at least when we were alone;*
2. *That I'd call him 'aap' (like how one addresses someone older) instead of 'tum' (like how one addresses someone younger or of the same age); and*
3. *That he'd treat me like a woman whenever possible.*

He agreed to the terms. He was drunk at the time.

I waited for him night after night, waited to hear the roar of his Yuvraaj bike, stayed up till one or two in the morning when he finally knocked.

'I'm very tired today.' He came in smelling of alcohol and lay prone on my bed.

'I'll massage you,' I offered.

He stripped and I poured Johnson's Baby Oil all over his back. I started with his thick, burly shoulders, huge enough to hold up the world. Soon, once I'd aroused him enough, he'd be upon me, wrapping his beefy arms around my body.

I moved down his back, the moles and scars I knew so well. I could tell him apart by those moles alone.

'Lower,' he mumbled.

I parted his buttocks, rubbed oil in the softness of his crack, felt the wetness on my penis. His buttocks had gooseflesh. Dot dot dot dot ... I poked each, counting them. I parted his buttocks and licked his crack. He rose on all fours, exposing his anus.

'Badhiya se chaat.' Lick well, he said.

I licked him wet, *lap lap lap lap*, inhaling his scent. I put my index finger into his anus and turned it around the soft inside.

'Ah! Ah!' he moaned in painful ecstasy. 'Ungli nahin, ungli nahin.' No finger, he begged.

We had sex again at six. He penetrated me and *prrrrr*—he farted. We laughed.

'You look beautiful,' he told me, tenderly, after he'd ejaculated.

I smiled.

'Boss,' he said.

'Why do you call me that?' I asked.

'Okay, sorry,' he said. 'Jaan.'

'Yes?'

'I need some money.'

'How much?'

'Two thousand.'

'Two thousand?' I turned towards him. 'I gave you that much two days back. Why do you want it?'

'I've borrowed some money from a friend,' he explained. 'I need to return it.'

'Okay,' I said. 'Take my card.'

He got out of the bed, naked, and extremely desirable. I took a good look at his back and buttocks in the diffused early morning sunlight. I wanted him, again. He took the ATM card from my wallet, dressed up, and left to get the cash. I lay there, naked, covered with my chadar.

When he returned after fifteen minutes, I said to him, 'You always talk about your friends. You never take me to meet them.'

'Why? Why do you want to see my friends?'

'Why shouldn't I?' I reasoned. 'After what we're doing I've got every right to meet whoever you meet.'

'They're not good people,' he said. 'They're gangsters, they've got guns.'

'And they'll shoot me, right?'

'You don't understand, jaanu.' He came and sat by my side, stroking my naked back. 'I can't let you meet them. It won't be right.'

'Forget me then,' I turned to the other side.

'Jaan,' he shook me.

'No.'

'Fine, I'll take you.'

'Today.'

'Today?'

'Yes, today.'

'Okay,' he said after a pause. 'Today.'

I waited the whole day. He didn't show up. I called him.

11.30 p.m. 'Some of my friends have been caught drinking on the road. I'm at the thana to get them released.'

12 midnight. 'I'm arranging money for their bail.'

12.45 a.m. 'I'm talking to the officer.'

1.15 a.m. No answer.

1.25 a.m. This number is busy. Please try later.

1.30 a.m. This number is switched off.

1.45 a.m. This number is switched off.

2 a.m. This number is switched off.

He came in the morning, sober, bathed, chewing Rajnigandha-Tulsi.

'Sorry, jaanu,' he says.

'Not this way,' I say. 'I'll meet your friends.'

'Look, it's not—'

'Either you take me or you leave.'

'Your duty?'

'I'm not going to work today. I'm going with you.'

He stood at the door, speechless, while I pretended to be busy.

'Okay,' he said meekly, and then he told me the rules. 'There, you are not to do what you do with me here.'

'What is that?'

'The place where we're going, the people there see me as a leader. I'm respected there. I have an image to maintain. And you have to give me some money.'

'Okay.'

The place was a dam resort some thirty kilometres outside the town. His friends, I saw, were from the proletariat. There was Nirmal's friend from school, a transporter who was a Karmakar; and four Adivasis who worked for him—two Santhals, a Munda and a Ho. We were later joined by a few students from a local engineering college and two of our juniors from the medical college. Except the transporter, each one called Nirmal 'Boss' or 'Deva'—someone who helps others, brings them happiness.

I wondered, what was Nirmal trying to do. Laying the field for the possible political career he so often boasted to me about? And what kind of respect was it if it came from a bunch of friends and yes-men?

The juniors were surprised to see me. They couldn't believe I had come with Nirmal.

'Aap yahaan?' they asked. 'You here? With Nirmal boss?'

I couldn't explain my presence.

'Yes, boss wanted to see this dam,' Nirmal said, yet they didn't seem entirely convinced.

Alcohol saved the day. After they started drinking, my presence was no longer an issue. I didn't drink; I wanted to stay in my senses, to observe, to take notes. They talked about the transport business, big money, women, wives, whores of Lachhipur. Nirmal and the transporter were the most boisterous of all, flaunting their political reach, their contacts with the police top brass. I was treated with respect because I was Nirmal's guest. I was given the best chair to sit on; a separate plate to have hors d'oeuvres from while they attacked the common platter; sealed packaged water bottles while they drank from jugs. What am I doing here? I wondered about my place in that unlikely company, my situation, how long I would be with Nirmal.

'Haraamkhor!' Nirmal was using his favourite expletive, laughing his loud, assertive laughter. 'I eat zinda maans! Live flesh!'

Sunit wasn't like this. He came from a family of politicians and philanthropists but there was a silent humility to Sunit, a determination to reach his goal without needing to talk about it or flaunting his contacts. Nirmal was the opposite. I heard him mumble in his sleep, an insecure soul inside that cocky body, living in the present, planning his survival second by second. He never slept peacefully. Sometimes he slept with his eyes open; sometimes on all fours after I rimmed him; sometimes with me sitting on top of him, riding his dick, pumping furiously, while he just snored.

I stuck to Nirmal's instructions, kept my hands off him. But when we sat down to dinner at a dhaba after the drinks, all of them made Nirmal and me sit separately on one side of the table while they sat across. Nirmal brought his chair close to mine. Smoking a Navy Cut, he placed his arm around me and squeezed my shoulder. I wondered if others were watching. Yes, they were, but they were busy with their backslapping and jokes. I removed his hand from my shoulder, putting on a straight face. Someone was playing a Sadri tune on a mobile phone.

Iskool kay tame pay, aana gori dame pay

Fair girl, bunk your school and meet me at the dam

Nirmal raised his bodybuilder's arms and waved them above his head. He knew I loved seeing him dance.

'What is that, boss?' one of our juniors asked.

'This is the Seraikella Chhau,' he grinned. 'A very famous dance form of our Seraikella district. I'm doing it for boss.' He put his arm around me.

'Looks like Salman's dance to me,' the junior said.

'Arrey, why not?' Nirmal said animatedly. 'I'm Salman. That *Tere Naam*, it is the story of my life.'

Annoyed at the mention of *Tere Naam*, I contorted my face.

'And here is my Katrina,' he whispered and kissed my ear. 'I hope you are not bored.'

'No.' I shook my head.

'How are you feeling?'

'Very happy.'

'You like my friends?'

'Yeah, but they're not dangerous at all.'

'You've seen nothing,' he grinned. 'That's why I was avoiding bringing you here.'

'I'd have come anyway.'

'Why?'

'Because I have this journalistic tendency. To know about people and places. To find stories.'

'Write something about me.'

'I've written already.'

'Yeah?' he smiled.

'Yeah.'

He lowered his head and kissed my neck.

Later, when I went to wash my hands, he came up and kissed me between my cheek and lips. None of his friends seemed to notice.

'Boss,' Nirmal told me one night, 'I want to do something with my life. I want to become a good man.'

'You will,' I ran my fingers through his hair.

'Jaan, will you keep on massaging me like this?' he asked.

'Marry me,' I said, 'and I'll live with you.'

'Only if you were really a woman,' he said tenderly, as if he meant it.

We are in my room. I talk to Nirmal in Oriya. He speaks that language in Seraikella, so I'm learning it to impress him.

'Kono koruchhi, agya?' I say.

'Kono koruchhonti, agya?' he corrects me in his sexy, masculine voice. 'Mottay mutto laguchhi.' He wants to pee.

'Aasontu, agya,' I tell him. Come, sir. 'Kori diyo.' Do it. I smile coquettishly, pull his jeans down, and take his thick penis in my mouth. He pees. Almost a litre. I drink it all. Then he gets naked.

His mobile rings. Midnight. Time for her to call. He grabs his jeans and, covering his crotch, rushes to a corner.

'Moti, you fatso!' he slurs into the phone, trying to sound sober. 'Had your dinner, love?'

I cover myself with the blanket and watch him fumble with his clothes, as if the girl he's talking to will jump out of the phone and catch him red-handed.

'Not slept yet? Why, love? ... Waiting for my call? ... Sorry, jaan, very sorry ... I was busy ... Had your medicines? ... Go to sleep, you have work in the morning ... I'll come to you soon, very soon.'

I blow him: a hurt, half-hearted blow job, because I can't live without sucking his dick. I massage his back as he snores. I check his call list. I see in his wallet the receipt for the watch that Moti has gifted him on his birthday, a Timex he wears at all times, even while fucking me.

I've shared with Nirmal my dream of attending a writers' residency in Puducherry. I've told him maybe we could both go to Puducherry one day, rent a sea-facing room in the Sea Side Guest House on the Goubert Avenue, and fuck as the sun rises from behind the Bay of Bengal. I've told him of my impossible desire to carry his baby inside me. I smell him in my sheets, in my breath. I've wondered if we could live together forever.

But no man will stay with me forever. They will all fuck me and forget me to settle down with women of their choice. Sunit left me. Nirmal will leave too. In fact, Nirmal will leave me the moment he finds a source of income and no longer needs me for money. I wish I could rip out my dick and balls and drill a cunt in me. But I can't become a woman, and I can't end it, and, in the morning, when he wakes up, we will fuck again.

'Aur zor se chodiye!' Fuck me harder! I will scream, tears rolling out of the corners of my eyes, something moving down my bowel. Shit, perhaps.

'Baarbhatari!' Nirmal will hiss, thrusting faster. 'How much harder?'

'Harder. So that it pains for years. And hit me. Please, hit me.'

He will pump his penis in and out, squeezing my breasts, kissing my back. I will raise my buttocks and counter his thrusts.

'Come on, come on,' I will hear him saying. He will slap my buttocks, pushing, panting. He will be smiling his intoxicated smile, but I won't turn around to look. Instead I will tell Nirmal to hit me harder, fuck me harder and not stop, to set my anus on fire, make it bleed, so that it will smart forever and remind me of him, long after he is gone.

F IS FOR FIRE

Abeer Hoque

Villazon

I met the firefighter in southern Bolivia, at the bus station in Villazon, a ramshackle deserted desert town on the border with Argentina. It was just after noon and the sun was burning off the last of the morning chill. The firefighter and his three companions were standing outside the station, wearing matching fake Adidas tracksuits, three in blue, one in red. More strikingly, they were all white, and much taller than any Bolivian. Then again, even as a brown one, so was I.

'Hauling four bags like so, is no way to live, dollface.'

'Could be she were moving house to here?'

'Aye, this town could do with some joy.'

I can apprehend or ape at least four English accents. Still, it took me a while to parse these cheerful insults, even longer to realize that they were being slung my way. The Australians and the Irish like nothing better than a good ragging, the more slangy and monkeyman, the better. The firefighter was not as jovially abusive as the other three. He was also the smallest quietest one. After greeting me sweetly, he returned to his book. I asked him what he was reading.

'*Anna Karenina*. My mum gave it to me. I'm rather liking it.'

Is it any wonder then that I fell instantly in love?

Tupiza

When the bus arrived, we got on and rumbled towards Tupiza. I sat beside the firefighter who told me he was taking a break from fighting forest fires in Tasmania to climb mountains wherever he could find them. Although right now, we were headed towards the salt flats—the famed Salar de Uyuni of Bolivia, an ancient salt lake that had dried up into the largest salt flats in the world. Four-day jeep tours headed out into the Salar from Tupiza, and by the time we got to Tupiza, the five of us had decided we would jeep together.

After dumping our things in a little hostel, we went in search of food and drink. I bought a bottle of cheap whiskey at a corner store on the way to the restaurant, and by the end of dinner, we were all properly smashed.

I talk a good talk, but when it comes to a crush, I'm tongue-tied. Liquor helps. On the stumbling walk back to the hostel, when I fell behind the others, and the firefighter asked me for a kiss behind the broke down pick up truck, I didn't hesitate. The sodium light turned us monochrome and his hands went exactly where I wanted them, just under my breasts, like underwire but better. I tried to hold his face but he shrugged my hands away. I settled on his belt loops, pulled his hips toward me. As his kiss deepened into my mouth, his hands shifted under my fleece, his thumbs flicking against my nipples. I hate that sensation. I love that sensation. It's too much and not enough.

We ended up at my dorm room in the hostel, which fortunately only had one other person in it, and unfortunately had one other person in it. Still, it was better than his dorm, which housed our multiple and ever mocking fellow travelers.

My twin bed was pushed up into the corner, two beds away from the other (hopefully deeply sleeping) occupant. There, under rough patterned Bolivian blankets, with all our clothes on, we kissed in quiet drunken abandon. Silent making out is the one of the hallmarks of youthful sex (no matter that we were both more than a decade into adulthood). It's exciting, forbidden, pre-intercoursal. It means I'll come.

I remember no details from that cold stuffy night, but somewhere in there, the caressing and the kissing and the grinding came together and I had my first orgasm with the firefighter. I felt it like a thin molten flame in my lower back. Then before I knew it, I was waking to an empty room in the hungover morning.

Next door, the others were also just rousing themselves. But where was the firefighter? Gone climbing, said the Irishman, giving me a thumbs up smile. But where?

I stepped out of the hostel, and in the blinding light of day, discovered what I had missed the night before. Tupiza is surrounded by mountains. And there was a tiny figure, in blue Adidas, halfway up one of the scrabbly rock faces.

By the time I showered and felt alive again, he was back. After his climb, he had gone to the market and brought back an avocado, a tomato, a chunk of cheese, and half a loaf of somewhat stale bread. We sat in the park on a bench in the sun, and I watched him cut everything up with his Leatherman knife. His hands were burned. Sinewed scars twisted up his arms under his clothes, reappeared at his throat, stopping just short of his jaw. I saw now why he had pushed my hands away from his face the night before.

One scar was so deep, it formed a smooth divot on the inside of his wrist. I reached out and touched it. My thumb fit perfectly inside the scar. He smiled, and handed me my breakfast.

'How you travelin?' he asked.

I couldn't be better.

Salar de Uyuni

Our jeep tour started the next day. By the time we climbed above 4000 metres, I was suffering from vise-like headaches, medium strength nausea, and the biting cold wind, despite the constant chewing of coca leaves and popping of altitude sickness pills. However, being above 4000 metres meant stunning mineral coloured lagoons, spiky mountain ranges, clouds of pink flamingos, and this last most alien surreal beautiful landscape: the Salar de Uyuni, a sea of hallucinogenic hexagonally-marked whitewhitewhite, as far as my awestruck eye could see.

I lay down on the flats, face down like a prayer. I licked the ground. Hard. Rough. Kind of salty. The firefighter crouched down beside me, pushed my hoody off my head, touched my electric hair.

'Where will you go after South America?' I asked, looking up at him. His thumb rubbed my lower lip. I bit it, forgetting my nausea for a second.

'Whistler, up in Canada,' he said, pushing his thumb into my mouth. I sucked. 'I'll find a night shift to work so I have my days free to climb.'

'Where will you live?' I asked, mouthful. In the distance, I could see a tiny brown island like a mole on a salt face. Giant cacti rose from its body like dinosaur spikes.

'In a tent.' He lay down beside me, replaced his thumb with his tongue. 'My mother is mailing it to me,' he said between cold kisses. Our breath hung as the white earth tilted. The blue sky fell all around.

I felt dizzy. I broke away and stood up. All sense of perspective disappeared in that expanse of white. The firefighter shot past me. I understood why. There was something about that landscape that either froze you dead, or propelled you like a star. He leapt high into the blue air.

I imagined it for a second. Looking for his tent in Whistler, finding it, staying. But it would never work. I had too many bags.

Potosi

No matter that we spent our days in a jeep carrying seven rowdy people, and our nights in shared shacks nestled in the howling landscape. No matter that the most we managed were exhausted kisses between sleeping bags just before passing out at night. The firefighter and I were having a full blown affair. Four days and my hands felt empty without his. Meals, bunk beds, backseats. We were magnetized, our bodies fitted to each other, side by clandestine side.

After the salt flat tour, we embarked on the worst bus ride I have ever taken: from Uyuni to the mining town of Potosi. Slated for five hours. Actual damage: eight. At night. On the most ruinous roads in the world. Every threadbare unreclining seat filled, plus every inch of aisle taken up by ticketless Bolivians, including the man sitting on my left foot. No heating or windows that closed properly. Music like cartoons on fast forward, on high volume of course.

But all of that means that your clever fingered lover can give you enormous pleasure in the crashbang dark. Totally unnoticed by anyone else.

Tongues and cocks are all very well, intimate, pleasurable, erotic. But there's something about the pressure and dexterity of fingers. Plus there's more than one. The firefighter was sitting beside me, as always, lounging against the frosty window pane, looking as if he were for all the world asleep. Still, he managed to get his icy left hand under my jeans, into my underwear. Two fingers winged past my clit, and then inside me.

The shock of cold was only my first undoing. His fingers soon warmed to burning, his rhythm an infuriating waltz. *Didn't he know I was a rock and roll kind of girl?* Four beats to a measure, and fuck if you modulate. Still I could feel his fingers slipping in and out more easily each time. Out. Tap. In. My body was going to take it, one way or another. Out. Tap. In.

As the feeling gathered between my legs, I could feel a slight burning sensation. Did I have to pee? Was it a UTI? Then I couldn't think anymore. Second hissing orgasm. I didn't even notice when the man sitting on my foot left the bus.

Sucre

Sucre, the quaint hilly red roofed sometime capital of Bolivia, had a cheap yummy market with fresh juices, a lovely textile museum, cafes with stellar views of the city, a sunny central plaza, pretty churches, affordable accommodations and dance clubs open all night every night. If you needed a place to rest after four days in a jeep and a horrible bus ride, this was it. We didn't want to leave.

On our second liver killing night in Sucre, a bunch of pretty ones joined us at the laser light nightclub. They flounced and pouted and sighed over the funny boys. I knew why. My crew was beautiful. Surfers, bikers, swimmers, hikers, climbers, adventurers all. Every last one had a lean body, distinct accent, and shining blue or green or grey or gold eyes.

'Firefighter, ever crash out coming down that pole?' asked the tall Australian construction worker in our group. He swigged his beer and batted his long lashes.

The girls giggled.

'I'm not that kind of firefighter,' he answered. 'I fight forest fires.'

'What fecking firefighter don't have a pole?' said the Irishman, giving him a thumbs down.

Bored with this line of questioning, they collectively turned their smiling charm on the girls, who responded by leaning in.

I got overdrunk and got gone, slipping out the back exit without telling anyone. To my dismay, the firefighter followed me. I didn't want him to see me all sorry and swerving. It turned out he wasn't following me. He was just trying to get home and he wasn't going to make it. At the doorway to our hotel, he passed out stone cold.

Crying, and cursing myself because usually I'm a happy drunk, I lifted him by his shoulders and dragged him across the courtyard and into our massive matrimonial room. In Bolivia, this is what they call the hotel rooms with one big bed. Still crying, I undressed him, and then myself. He was thin, strong, and pale, his body boneless and heavy in his state. I couldn't see his scars, but I could feel them under my hands. I traced them down to where they ended, past the birdcage of his ribs, below his fingertips.

'Why am I doing this?' I wept out loud. 'When you don't even know. When you won't even remember.'

His cock was useless, a sweet soft thing. I lowered my mouth and licked him. I had lost my hairclip and my hair figured into everything. But because I was moving at lava speed, it didn't matter. I could push my slow motion hair away just as slowly. Unconscious, he grew under my tongue.

I have always found the metamorphosis from flaccid to erect astounding, absurd. Here the helmet, one eye weeping. There the ridges, the pulsing vein. And below, the soft taut sack.

My tears fell in the hollows of his hips, rolled off his body, and disappeared. I kept sucking until it became a dream.

I awoke in sunlight with naked sticky skin, hair like a monster. The firefighter was leaning against the carved wooden headboard, watching me. He handed me a bottle of water. I drank like I was dying.

'You're sommat else,' he said, running his scarred hand over my stomach, past my breast, along my collarbone, stopping at my throat. Blood pounded through my aching head. The nipple he had grazed briefly hardened like a betrayal. He lifted his hand and stared. 'Crackin.'

I thought maybe that was a compliment.

La Paz

After two weeks of heavy breathing all over Bolivia, I thought I'd have acclimated to the altitude a bit. But no. I couldn't walk a block in La Paz without getting huffy-puffy. The airport was 4000 metres in the sky and the drive alone down to town was worth it all. Our taxi careered down the mountains surrounding the city. Everywhere you looked, the slopes were dotted with houses, the way you'd expect to see tree cover.

The giant Aussie wasted no time figuring out how to get our vitamins. La Paz's coke dens were alive and tripping. Club 36 was an unmarked joint that only opened at midnight. After two false starts and some awkward Spanish, we found it, by going through a fake apartment in a shady neighbourhood, down the stairs into the basement, and through a long narrow hallway.

There in the dim light were groups of fiends chattering on couches, leaning over low coffee tables. The orders came on trays, the cocaine arranged neatly inside clear baggies, short straws, and sharp dividers, all at a fraction of the going rate anywhere in the Western world.

I don't like coke. It's pricy and lasts a split. And it's the opposite of ecstasy, turning people greedy and small. But in Club 36, with the firefighter cutting our shares, pressing his thumb into my hot palm, I didn't care. Probably because I didn't care about anybody right then, not even him. Everyone was talking a mile a minute. The conversation, normally funny sharp, turned sharp sharp. The more we cut, the more we laughed. At each other.

Six hours later, we emerged from the den into the pale dawn and huffed back to our hotel. As he opened our room door with an oversized brass key, he looked at me.

'Your nose is bleeding,' he said, unhurried, unworried.

I walked in and looked in the armoire mirror and saw a tiny red snake coming out of my nose. He wound one arm around my waist from behind, and with the other hand, wiped the blood off with his thumb.

As I leaned back, time stopped, and that image of us froze in my mind like a photograph. His bloody thumb, my smeared upper lip, his arms around my body, our flashing eyes.

In the next photograph, the curtains are drawn and we're in bed. For hours and hours, we hold hands and toss and turn, into each other, away from each other.

Every time we kiss, or I sit up for a drink of water, I think my heart will pound out of my chest. Cheap coke and high altitude. Bolivian hearts must be tougher than most.

My last night in La Paz was also my last night with the funny boys. I was heading west to Machu Pichu, and the rest of them, including the firefighter, were going north to the Amazon. We had the lamp lit hotel room to ourselves and a window that ate up an entire wall, overlooking a steep cobblestone street.

Naked and lazy, we kissed for an hour, and then another. If you look at your lover every day for two weeks, you memorize certain things. Like the crinkling around his eyes that means that he's tired. Or the lower lip bite when he's thinking about touching you. I could enjoy each of these madeleines, because I didn't really believe it was our last night together. As corporeal as the last fourteen days had been, they had also been instantly nostalgic, instagram retro, unreal.

'What's this now?' he asked, pulling a silky bag from under my pillow. He looked at me, biting his lip.

'My vibrator,' I said grinning past my embarrassment.

'You mind if we use it?' he asked, unveiling its blue curved body.

I shook my head.

'Beauty. Spread your legs,' he said.

'Okay, but I want you after. You, not just some silicone shaft.'

'You'll get what you want,' he said.

He reached down with his hand without looking and found my pussy in the first go. Heading downward, he started to lick me slick, holding the lips open with his fingers. When I had just hit my rock rhythm, despite his three step, he straightened up and put the vibrator in his mouth, deep and wet, in and then out, easy and slow. Had my firefighter practiced with the other team? My belly clenched in arousal and jealousy.

He pushed the vibrator inside me, something I rarely did since the vibrations against my clit were usually more than enough. It felt too full too fast, but nothing to complain about. He switched it on, and the rabbit ears next to my clit fluttered to life, pearls pulsing in the shaft inside me. My body weakened to jelly in seconds. The humming in my clit strung out in all directions. I no longer knew where my body started or the feeling ended.

When he let the vibe go, and lay on top of me to bite at my breasts, I turned liquid. The rabbit ears throbbed valiantly below his weight. He left my breasts for my mouth, sucking my tongue like he had just found it, the thing he had been looking for in the fire.

It was then that I came, in a paroxysm of pleasure, my last searing orgasm with the firefighter. I arched away from him, into the thin cool air, insensible, in flight.

Beyond the window were the lights of La Paz, tiny man-made stars pricking Bolivia's dark earth body. Her silent mountains loomed and then fell away to the south, a vast sea of salt and rock lapping at her toes.

THE PERISCOPE

Lopa Ghosh

Ila is at a market, bending over radishes, when I decide to periscope her at night. From my vague newspaper memory I know who she is. Frost gathers on her hair like a shower of diamonds. As she walks through the market, her courtesan hips sing like spring. Ila is in the smell, the wetness, the filthy city fog. She is in the deepest recesses of imagination. In the evening, I visit her house of glass and mirrors. She wears an eggplant kanjeevaram like a river still warm with the memory of sun, braided, slung and draped to deepen the shadows and swells. She gets up and pours out a song on the stereo. Her pallu shifts and the world tilts with it. Music ripples through the house full of lovers. Advait is a fat man in a pink shirt who grins at Sarna, the girl with a rose tucked in high white boots. Advait is ungainly on his knees, but he bends and does as expected—teeth-clasps the rose. The rose falls but his face is where it should be. Sarna's tight little skirt cannot hold back the forest smell. In the garish light of a chandelier directly atop their sprawl, Sarna's white boots glisten, the rise of her breasts starkly lit like those of a Manet slut. Soon Advait is headless. I turn now to the others around me. Virendra takes apart Pinky, bit by bit, coaxing her into a slow loving. She is ready to crumble while he folds his hands like a water bearer to receive her. Then he whispers that the lights are too bright, they must seek out their own patch of grass. So she picks up the choli she has let drop and, sheltered under his hooded eyes and her silk dupatta, runs off with him into one of the many boudoirs Ila has decorated for love. Pinky's eyes shine when Virendra lifts her rustling ghagra, tears her golden panty into shreds, leaving on a skeleton of it, as if to taunt her nakedness more. Her breasts are bare under the veil. Leave it on, he says, and hoists her onto a console by the window. I leave them at that and return to the room of chandeliers where Sarna's hips are deafening. They dance and plunge soaking Advait's stiff and trembling rod with unmeasurable hotness. I stay briefly, mesmerized by the rhythm, then run out again to seek Ila and discover her pleasures. My body trembles as I periscope through the house. In the bar, an MP lies face down on Rupa's belly while she catches up on her sleep. His erection is lying sideways, half wilted. He has slept off too early. I hope she will run. I hope she will get the money.

I have discovered fortuitously that soul is a cake. You can eat it and have it too. So I break off a little from my soul cake and barter it for a periscope. It happens suddenly. Sunny morning, baby gurgling in the pram, tree shadows on the still water of a Sultan's tank, imagined echoes of the Hindu queen's anklet as she teases the water, her muffled moans under the Sultan's crushing lips. I am withdrawing into myself when the chance of bartering an extraordinary periscope presents itself and I grab it. No, not a submarine scrap with Russian inscriptions. It could be a nom de guerre for magic or a synecdoche. But such petty considerations I dispel quickly and take home the lust sweller—a long hollow tube, entirely collapsible and smelling of ocean (possibly mildew but much nicer to think otherwise).

Wind under my coat, I wheel the baby away from the lake where darkness is gathering, and start the car. A song on the radio and the baby's squeals of delight add music to the thrill of possessing the periscope. Little magnets spin in my forehead and on my fingers. The house is warm, the wood shines, candles flame their welcome, underfoot the woollen rugs gift me memories. But soon after the skies open up and let loose a hail storm. The cold becomes a person. The baby wakes up. I toast coconut oil with camphor on the stove and rub the warm and fragrant oil on its little toes.

As night grows, whispers from my skin naked under the nightgown call out to the dark corners of the house and soon they sit, the shadows and my soliloquies, sharing secrets, lighting candles, cooking meals for a lover who will clasp their breasts and drink from them. The lascivious tongue of that stranger lashes at my little settlement. I walk the stairs and the corridors in a yellow fog nightgown, my breasts heavy and flowing, my feet on fire.

Into the night I train the periscope and look for secrets of love. First few times are odd, jerky. Once I land inside a Buick, under Marilyn Monroe's skirt. I discover that Shah Jahan has the face of a man who lives on the tenth floor of my apartment building and has recently lost his job. I stay for a while as in his fancy, the costumes that the women wear are splendid, ornate yet sheer, a wisp of air held together by jewels and exit only after a slave girl faints. My eyes adjust to the undersea of secrets. I travel regardless of time or compass. My body fills up with new stories, swells, rises, floats, shudders.

I learn quickly and soon I am a nimble traveller. At Ila's house I glide, adjusting focus, zooming in, choosing pleasure and pleasure-seekers at my own will. I keep the best for the last—Ila the goddess, the master artisan of a commune of orgy—what pleases her I wonder. But Ila is not with the kingmaker either. Nor is she with the economist who has gone home to his wife. Finally I find her behind large doors of sandalwood on a bed of silk. The room smells of roses, enveloped in dense trees. The eggplant kanjeevaram lies neatly folded, the blouse wrapped around it. They have been kept out to be aired. On a large bed embroidered with rust leaves, Ila sleeps soundly, a pillow between her legs. The lucid muscles of her face invite my borrowed fantasy to dissolve itself. The periscope retracts and I lie down next to the woolly giraffe.

The city is a river of lust. Little boats of orgy sail past my house. Sometimes they wave at me when I sit on the window cooing to the baby. Hello mother. Hello wife. How about a quickie while the baby sleeps? Feed us. Take us in your mouth. But no one steps out of the boat. Curtains of lace, my bordello face, cannot disguise the monastic gloom of my house. Often when the periscope is resting I long to be crushed by him. A gash from a knife, the pinch of a tight dress under the armpit, a rough wall grazing my bare back, the burn of perfume on naked skin, the baby's toughened gum, inevitably become his hands, upturned coarse palms, the knots on his fingers, the sunburn on his cheeks.

The baby is six months old today and I am yet to celebrate its birth, its coming into my life. I pour myself wine and sit by the lamp which has a geisha on its papery walls, hoping, that while it sleeps under the tiger, crocodile and whale, my friends, my dearly beloveds, the music and merrymakers for the party that I have planned, will find my new blue door and knock. Knock knock!

Since I gave birth, it is as if the pain is finished and I have nothing more to turn to inside me. The wine glass, I twirl around its stem, tilt the mercurial lake to the left, hoping to discover the staircase that will lead me in. And then the baby cries out in a dream, I imagine, of the cat who threatens to eat the pumpkin, or more practical and visceral, because it misses sliding its fingers along the walls of my uterus, it misses the snakey placenta, swimming with it, coiling up next to it. But the baby cries and I am taken away, once again to a happiness that pre-empts the existence of words, cast against each other yet harmonious, bearing away a Gulliver on their ant heads.

Ro has invited me to a party.

Come, he says. You will see it's fun.

I call the baby's grandmother and ask her if she would babysit for an evening. It will be amusing I tell her. The baby has eyes like her son.

I don't care, she says. After a point or after three grandchildren it's pretty repetitive. But it's okay. I will look after the baby for a night. The dog might like a distraction.

So I go, the summer breeze in my hair, the smell of ash on my fingers, the long forgotten stickiness of outside on my breasts. I am wearing white with little orange flowers which glow like fireflies on my thighs when I stand against the light. Ro kisses me hard after we park outside the house where music thumps on the terrace. He slides the dress off my shoulder, buries his head in my chest. My body is full of knowing and he senses it.

Wow, he says, after a while. You are so full today.

I climb the stairs throbbing with a strange joy. My body has known and endured a pain created by the gods. People don't say it much, but let it be known, I think, that giving birth is an aphrodisiac. And the periscope is my prize. It snuggles at my waist unseen under the thin dress, becoming one with the shadows. Ro is now firm and heavy but I move on in search of the others. Some of them kiss rather well. They adore my dress and make me stand above the candles lined along the wall. Mukhtar entertains me best with stories of his recent photographic assignment with the tribals. He speaks at length about the marvellous effects of struggle on muscle tone. So I lift my raptorial leg and make him run his hand over my inner thigh. I tell him I can hold his head between and crush the cranial bone to smithereens. He looks quite mad and says in a hot whisper, whip me.

I play cunny squeezing with Arg who has begun to intrigue me. I hear the story of how he was cuckolded by his own friend Shyam from Shyam's wife Mita. Mita's loveliness I have touched and discovered when we raced through those mojitos and revealed secrets to each other. They are all here today—Arg, his wife Sheetal, Shyam who fucked Sheetal and Mita, Shyam's wife. Later Arg brings me a glass of wine and says it works smoothly with mojito. Trust me.

We take our glasses and sit on the stairs. Arg's hands toy with the anklet on my feet and then slowly creep up, twirling, pinching, making little eddies on my naked flesh. He teases me with abeyance—prolonging, touching, forgetting, beckoning my cunt. His fingers weave a filigree of feather grazing, simmering distance, hard piercing. Fucking non fucking drives me to a frenzy. I ache, I melt into a thick warm trickle. Then he calls it cunny and says it's the wettest he has ever had. I lean back and open myself further to him. I hear Sheetal tinkling in another corner. She has worn a clever ensemble of sheerness—peach, gold, white and silver—it covers her nipples but throws their hardness to sharp relief, clothes her navel but deepens its shadow, flows between her legs but as a reminder of what lurks. Sheetal sways over to Shyam who had fucked her in the kitchen and then fucked her again standing in an elevator ten years ago. I close my eyes when Arg's finger slides inside me. He gasps at my wetness and swears he is going to make me come right there. In the cinema of my shut-eyes, my periscope brings me images of Sheetal and Shyam's kitchen-fuck and elevator-fuck. When the cuckolding happened Sheetal was not yet married to Arg. Shyam was passing through the city. In the afternoon when the other friends had left, Sheetal walked into the kitchen where Shyam was making tea, her small, tight breasts and erect nipples arrogant under her white t-shirt. Through the periscope I see her bent over as Shyam squeezes her bare ass, snakes his hand down at the front and twiddles her nipples. Later in the elevator, Shyam presses down on the STOP button and kisses her hard, she goes down to suck him.

Arg responds to my cunny's demands to quicken his pace. He curves his finger, breaking through the waterfall into the summer palace while I watch him being cuckolded ten years back. In my head I carry the fantasies of a crowd, the sun of a splendid orgy.

I take the baby for a walk. It sits in the pram and squints when the sun shines full on its face. A lower incisor is causing trouble which I try to soothe with Arnica and a frozen hanky to chew on. From every corner of the world around me, I purloin jewels. Such as the peculiar aesthetics of a telecom wizard. One night, soon after Damien Hirst stuffed a young antelope with formaldehyde, sawed off its horns, replaced them with gold and called it the Golden Calf, I happened to periscope through D. Seth's grand bungalow. I find him in the oak-lined study with three young girls. They are tall and thin and wear nothing but, like a tree bark around their waist, Picasso's little known pen and ink sketches of a prostitute.

Another afternoon I learn that Jagath the poet writes his verses at the back of Geeta's bookshop. I am thumbing through the new Murakami. There are no customers. Geeta plays with the baby for a while and encourages me to look at the poster selection. When I look up from posters of Green Peace, Geeta has slid into the closet of poems. Jagath is as pale as ice and pitifully boney against Gita's soft corners and warm brown skin. Through the thwerp and suck of pelvis and skin, I travel into an orgy of film stars that Jagath is building up in his mind while he rides Geeta. He slaps their tight ass, his cold face buried in their sex, as they dance to a loud Hindi song. Katrina Kaif and Madhuri Dixit shimmy their bosoms on his face. They wear tight cholis tied at the back with strings. A tall girl (I don't recognize) in a short skirt bends over on a large desk. Jagath turns from Madhuri's bosom to the girl on the desk, her thongs disappearing in the dark valley and then back to Madhuri again. Suddenly the scene changes and Jagath is in a lovely green lawn where Shilpa Shetty is lying on the grass, her waist lifted in the air. She is in black leotards and twists herself into complex asanas, revealing a perfect camel toe.

The rains have come. I dance when no one is looking, my feet relish the wet grass. The baby is in the buggy under a tree. I wave at it and then lose myself to the clouds. When I turn back Vyom is under the tree, shielding the baby from the rain that now drums louder, harder. That stranger I befriend and we run back home together. I get to know that he lives on the floor above and feel exceedingly glad that the first time I see him is not through my periscope eyes. Son of a priest, Vyom has left his hometown for good. The gods are too interfering he says. I invite him to dine with me and studiously ignore the tug and pull of my periscope. Vyom is mine to discover. I want to build a new fantasy, fresh, free of the past, luminous in its own sensuality. After the simple yet suggestive supper, I pour him another scotch and prepare to kiss him. Vyom is breathtaking. His eyes are pained and unfocussed. I sit on his lap and nibble on his lower lip which tastes of faraway islands. And then he requests me to stop and says it's not that I don't want you—which I believe as he is unconsciously sliding his hands over my breasts and stroking my nipples—but I cannot do this. I am sick, sick to the core he says and goes home.

Tonight I have come far away to the sickle moon city. In the darkness of pre-dawn Shiva will be roused. There is not a soul except the priests, portly Shaivites who fondly laugh at the interfering rat, calling him dearly beloved son, a few monkeys who hang from the sky and a tremulous young girl who has come to invite Shiva to her wedding. My periscope eyes wait for Vyom to appear. The girl is scared of the monkeys so the priests invite her into the sanctum sanctorum. Shiva sleeps here, when he is not everywhere else. In that little altar, he curls up, folds back his priapic energy and lets the fat Brahmins rouse him every morning with bhaang, flowers and milk. I can lie down right there with my periscope, my cheek against Shiva's and spend the night pillow talking, shape shifting.

Far away at the edge of a labyrinth I hear a motorbike roar to a halt. Footsteps reverberate through the winding alleys. Vyom's approach thunders through my heart. Soon he is at the threshold, his body wound tight, simmering with resolve. The round Brahmins sing gentle songs, grind the bhaang and knead the ganja. The chillum is polished till it shines. Shiva's eternal tumescence is bathed in a river of milk and rubbed with turmeric. Smeared with sandalwood the ancient black rock glows. One garland after another is placed on it, till the hardness is lost in a soft ambrosial sheath. When Shiva has been appeased and caressed awake, the arati begins.

The young girl shivers in the biting cold. I can smell the river in her wet hair. She holds out a wedding card and a large pot of sweets to the priests who whisper a word on her behalf to the Lord. He will come, they say, and bless her.

Vyom is suddenly aware of her. The perfect waist, soft neck and tender feet stir him. The girl turns and they stand next to each other. Shiva goes to sleep again and they silently leave his abode. In purple light the girl puts her head on Vyom's shoulder. They have come to greet the sun on the steps by the river. A pyre is burning but there are no mourners. They have gone to warm themselves with a cup of tea. Shiva is sulking in the river mist, waiting for the flesh to dissolve, the bone cage to break. He will accost the soul when it breaks free. But till then he has time to bite his lower lip and wonder at destiny. He glances at Vyom and the girl. They kiss. Vyom brushes his thumb over her nipple, hard as marbles, yet as fresh as the dew-soaked froth of milk the city was famous for. He holds her breasts aloft to the song floating in from the river. They rise together to a crescendo, the song and the breasts. He whistles warm circles into her skin, wet, sandy and cold from the breeze.

The boatman, who could be a courtesan's son, takes his music upstream. That little rush has passed and so has Vyom's feathery playfulness. Her face, latticed with wet hair, radiates a sweet piousness. On her forehead, the vermillion that the priests blessed her with is smudged.

Thin flowers of gold glisten at her neck and ears. These giveaways of purity, of betrothal and obeisance dare him to perpetrate. Yet she wants to be loved and this assures him as he lays his head on her bare navel. He sucks the vestigial crevice, unheeding of ash that has floated in from Shiva's lonely smoke and settled in the folds.

Early morning bathers could arrive soon. So he shelters her in a darker corner and sits her on the steps. Deep inside she is warm and moist, her curls still wet from the morning dip in the river. His tongue gets heavy with turmeric and the sweetly revolting taste of the river. He pulls her to her feet. They run like wind and ride out on the motorcycle. The young girl guides him silently, pointing with her fingers, asking him to slow down or take a turn with the pressure of her hand on his thigh. They stop outside an old mansion decorated with streams of lights, their brightness dimmed in the gathering light of dawn. Large awnings of red and gold have been unfurled. A makeshift platform has been erected for shehnai players.

Vyom holds her back. He doesn't trust this anymore.

No, trust me, she says.

They tiptoe across the sleeping house. The wedding is two days away and people are exhausted. Snores, coughs, feet shuffles, sleep talks drown out the heaviness of their lust. Inside the girl's room, Vyom presses himself against her. He pulls off the wet saree. She stands there with high breasts and a belly as smooth as a leaf. Vyom spreads her wide and stares at a new possibility. In the half-light of morning she lets herself be mauled. He bites her soft flesh, buries his fingers and tongue in every crevice he can find. She moans softly and goads his mouth to her breasts, her thighs, the inside of her elbow, her wrist, the back of her knee. The bed makes so much noise that Vyom spreads a thick blanket on the floor. But they are dancers today so they resist lying down. She impales herself on Vyom, her legs wrapped around his waist. They spin and spin till he finds himself meteoring to the sky. The debris of their love is smeared with virginal blood.

She thanks him and lowers her eyes. He wants to make her happy. But she says he already has. No literally, you know I can make you ... he presses his fingers into her dampness. She shudders but shakes her head. He gently caresses and says let me. No no, she says. You have made me happy.

When? He is surprised.

Twice, she says, and smiles shyly her eyes lingering on his face.

Vyom wants to kiss her once more. His heart is turning over and he is scared that it may hurt later. But she has shut herself from him. Leave, she says and pushes him out of the room.

Vyom runs down the stairs, leaping over four at a time. He has half-crossed the courtyard when he runs into a man who is probably the girl's father. Vyom has nowhere to run. He considers saying he entered the house by mistake or that he is a thief looking for heirlooms in old mansions. But the man smiles up at him and thanks him profusely. He leads Vyom into the kitchen and requests him to have a sweet and a glass of water. Then he holds out a small tray of shagun, laid out with sweets, haldi, tika, and silver coins. For you, please accept.

At the chowk where all the streets converge, sweetmakers bring indoors the thickened milk left overnight under the sky. I see it become gold when flavoured with saffron. Strong arms churn and churn till all that is left of the milk is froth. I name the girl, who Vyom has defiled under Shiva's watchful gaze, Nimmish after the delicacy and my throat is lumpy with the sweetness of sudden love.

In the kitchen when I bake apples, the orange sun comes to tease my shoulders. I long to bare them instead to rough hands. I wait for dusk, a snatch of sleep, a tongue on the back of my knee, orange pekoe tea, moonshine, the son of a priest, shoe polish, and many such tiny peccadilloes. In another room, where I travel at night, a king is about to lose his throne because a maid has bent over to make tea. Silver spoon scrapes fragile china. The hypnotic swirl of cream in coffee takes too long to dissolve. Under the white apron, bordered with pretty frills, lush boobs rise to be kissed. Afterwards I stroll through Paris, where the king has had his fall, and observe to myself that sex without loved-ness is the reason planets turn and make music daily, eternally.

The baby born out of once loved-ness has been gently rocked to sleep. Years of love-toil and love-tears have been erased and now there is no memory left of shoulder blades that glistened like magic mountains in the dark. But now I can spin. Spin and spin and spin and wait for my kingdom to come.

THE MATINEE

Mohan Sikka

At four o'clock, the lights at Sylvan Talkies fade to black. A crackle in the air, as the ancient projector rolls, announces *Secret Love*, the romantic release that's been sending up the 'house full' signs this monsoon season. The notes of the first song and dance begin to play, and a whooping, joyful cry rises from the seats—it's the radio hit that's on everyone's lips. The clapping and stomping subside, clouds roll on the screen from four directions, timed to lilting music and the drumbeat of thunder, and the rain starts to fall, little drops at first, then great pouring streams from the sky, and a man with a cocky top hat and a crooked cane and white shoes sings and dances all around a woman in a drenched, very tight sari, her hair limp as an oily noodle but her mascara unyielding, her face turned away from the man, impervious to his serenade. Then the lightning flashes so bright that the man on the screen disappears for a second—bleached white—and the clouds make such a tremendous fireclap that the lusty boys in the audience scream with delight, and the heroine's pretty eyes and mouth open extra wide as she holds up her hands and runs to the man. The lowest theatre doors under the blue exit signs swing open with fury, crashing against their stoppers, and a surge of outdoor air, smelling of hailstorms and wet earth, comes rushing in to fill the musty space. For a second, there is wonder in many eyes—*what an amazing film effect!*—but the boys are soon laughing at their easy mistake, as the ushers run down the aisles and muscle the swaying doors shut, and others run up to the lobby to close the windows against the real storm trying to force its way inside. All eyes return to the dark screen; to the phantom rain clouds and the synthetic streaks of lightning; to the woman, more amenable now to the dancing man's attentions.

A small boy of eleven shivers in his seat. Cousin-Brother and he were late, and caught some of the early showers on the pavement while Cousin-Brother bargained with a shark for three tickets to the sold-out show. The boy's cotton half-shirt is wet, his khaki shorts are damp, the handkerchief in his pocket soggy from sniffling.

'*Aaaaa ... chooooo!*' he sneezes, raining fine drops of snot on the seat in front of him, too late to dig out his hanky.

'Arrrrreeey, quiet! ... Movie's on ... Shhhhhhh!!! ... Take it outside!' voices respond from all around.

'Brother, I have to go to the toilet,' the boy says, in a tiny voice. He wanted to speak up earlier, but did not want to bother his cousin during the rush to find seats. He worships this older cousin, who attends the university and lives with the boy's family. For the boy this outing is the highlight of his week.

Cousin-Brother frowns. Seema wasn't waiting outside the ticket window as she had promised. The gel in his long, styled hair is flat now, from the rain and from running his hands repeatedly through his substantial mane. The necessity of bringing the boy along to satisfy his aunt will not be compensated by sneaked tender touches and handholding with his girlfriend. Tomorrow, he will have to concoct stories of seduction to share with his cricket buddies in college. *And* he had to shell out fifty rupees from his meagre pocket money for her fucking ticket. Dammit!

Pinching the boy's ear, he says: 'Didn't Aunty tell you to go before we left the house? This is the last time I'm taking you to a picture. She can send you with the servant from now on. Now bloody well sit still and wait for the intermission.'

The boy nurses his burning ear. 'Brother, please, have to go very badly.'

'I said, just hold it.' Cousin-Brother turns his face away, unsympathetic.

And the boy does, somehow, twisting and turning in his pants, pressing down on his thighs with his hands, tightening and releasing his abdominal muscles. *I shouldn't have gotten involved with her,* Cousin-Brother thinks, glowering at the screen. *What an ass I am. People told me she was a tease. They warned me.*

The man and woman in the film confront a set of awkward decisions: the woman's father turns out to be the villain that our hero, a police detective, has been chasing since the murder of his family. How can he love her now—a criminal's daughter, the scion of an outlaw responsible for his own childhood tragedy? She could be a criminal herself, inheriting her father's tendencies. But wait. Is the villain *really* her father ... *or the father's twin brother separated at birth?* How can we tell? Will the hero find out before it's too late? ... ALL WILL BE REVEALED AFTER INTERMISSION.

The image on the screen folds and the drapes close over the stage. Cousin-Brother continues staring bleakly ahead, his eyes grey and clouded.

The boy is squirming violently now, and whimpering. 'Brother, please, Brother, please, Brother. I *have* to go. Brother, are you listening?' He prods his cousin's leg with a crumpled fist.

Cousin-Brother jerks back to life. '*Go* then, motherfucker, go,' he snaps. 'Get up! ... I'll follow you in a minute.'

'You have to come with me.' The boy has never used public toilets alone.

'Don't be a baby. This is why you get called a little girl. I said I'm coming. Go!'

The boy rises uncertainly, and asks an usher for directions. Following his cursory gesture, he hobbles down the sloping aisle to the front of the theatre. By the time he reaches the first few rows he is almost running. He takes the narrow gap between the first and second rows, scrambling past seated patrons, beating out the crowd heading to the left exit through the passageway. Outside the door he's in a stairwell. He scampers up a flight of stairs, and finds himself in front of the ladies' bathroom. He asks another lolling usher about the men's toilet, then skips down two floors, his heart beating clear out of his chest, and sees his destination at last.

His mistake has cost him precious time. The line for entry curves around the corner. He joins the end of it, legs trembling with his last reserves of restraint. Ahead of him are shuffling men and boys, in grey and drab brown and dark blue pants, heads down, hands in pockets, minds focused by tight bladders. This silent, snaking assembly winds gradually towards its objective. The moments pass, and the need becomes too desperate for some—these ones groan and break off from the queue, and hurry down one more flight to the ground level exit for instant gratification against a wall or tree trunk. Those less close to breaking point resign themselves to waiting their turn.

Entering the door of the toilet, a potent whiff of yellow vapour assails the senses, and this eliminates some of the less hardy as well. For the rest, a few more steps, and then a final, happy arrival!—a rapid unzipping or unbuttoning along trough-like urinals on opposite sides of the room, the urinals once gleaming white, now painted in a palette of yellows and rusts and mould-greens. At the troughs, on a low platform, the men and boys stand in a variety of poses: some stare down, very focused; some look upwards; others stand loosely, humming; and one or two are frankly curious, eyes darting this way and that. If there was fresh water flowing freely, a healthy gurgle from the inlet and outlet pipes, one could by force of will imagine standing over a stream in an open field. Given the mean trickle seeping from the inlet, however, and the splashing, steaming piss pooling over the half-clogged drain, the effect is closer to tipping at the brink of a noxious cauldron.

This kind of communal basin is unfamiliar to the boy. It mocks his desperation, his long-teased bashfulness in even using a regular urinal. The crush of men behind him brings him right to the rim of the trough. His bladder is beyond the point of bursting. His hands are sweaty. He stands there for some moments, unable to act. To the right of him a gentleman with a large belly says, 'Come on, come on, take it out.' And then, smirking slightly: 'Needing some assistance? Where is your Papa? Feeling shame-shame?'

The boy shakes his head shyly, No. Slowly, he reaches for the front of his shorts, cheeks flushed, eyes straight ahead. There are few boys his age around, and none unaccompanied. He wishes Cousin-Brother was here, even though openly peeing next to him is a shame-inducing thought. He wishes that he did not have to go so bad. He unzips himself and digs his fingers inside his still damp underwear, pulls out his penis and leans over the trough. As his bladder muscles contract, he shivers involuntarily, with an immense, immeasurable relief, the kind of relief that cannot believe the finishing line has been reached without an accident. He pees for a long time, the longest time, it seems to him, he has ever needed to pee.

In his social studies period at his very special school, his geography teacher shows an animal movie every Friday. She has a betel nut addiction, along with a mighty thirst for Campa Cola with ice on unbearable early afternoons in May, weeks before the monsoon is scheduled to arrive. Her imagination is worn down by the temperature, and so she fires up her old classroom projector, and starts the film, *An Elephant Sleeps*—the same one every time—her mind so hungry for the betel nut and the cola that she skips entirely the tired question: *Boys, Have I shown you the Jungle Safari picture?* and turns on the reel just anywhere before escaping to the teachers' lounge. A whitewashed classroom wall becomes a screen on which the cracked, bleached out images play, while the audience torments its weakest members, including the boy, with bits of broken chalk. A man's rich, hushed voice provides occasional commentary as drinking elephants slake their fierce thirst on the African savannah, dipping their long, languorous snouts into the waterhole, the water not sparkling blue or green like the ocean, but red and brown and yellow, picking up colours from the soil around it. The boy has seen the movie so many times he remembers the elephants' names.

Lined up at the trough, the boy realizes, with the sudden pleasure of recognition, are men-elephants, elephant-men, trunks dangling: some large and fat, flaring violently; some small and barely peeping; some skinny, unbelievably lengthy; some hooded; some pulled back. All the elephant-men are making their peace with the breaking and drawing of water, some breathing noises of release and contentment, *aaaaaaah*, others shaking their trunks at the end, before raising and retracting them. The mood of the herd increases the boy's own sense of well-being as he pees, the previous awful sensation of being engorged replaced with a pleasant, almost sweet emptiness. As the boy's piss ends but he has not yet pulled away himself, waiting for the last errant drops to fall from his penis in his hand, he becomes aware of a new sensation. He thinks at first that some pee is left inside him still. He tightens and releases his groin muscles but nothing emerges from the tip of his penis. Instead, the sensation catches and becomes more intense, something between an ache and a tingle, located at once along his penis and somewhere behind it, inside his lower belly, a tingling way down below his navel, related to and also distinct from the relief of emptying his bladder. The boy shudders and the feeling reaches, as an extended frisson, all through his body. His small penis begins to rise as if saluting the other elephants, and the tingling grows in force and is wonderful; the touch of his own hand feels different, charged, as if his fingers possessed magical powers, and his penis were a wand with sparks and little bursts of light, instead of piss, spurting from its hole. He is struck by this, lost in the strange novelty of it, no words or memory in his mind to relate to what is happening, when he realizes that the big-bellied gentleman who teased him has disappeared, and that a second pair of eyes is watching him closely from above, just to his right. A stranger with a long face, closely shaved, and a fierce, almost alarmed, expression.

Suddenly self-conscious, the boy jerks back. Stepping away from the trough, he fumbles and zips his shorts. He looks for a sink. There are two around the corner, in a small adjacent space, facing a row of emptying toilet stalls. He shuffles over to the first cracked sink and checks the faucet, but there's no water. The faucet on the second sink has no handle. He wipes his hands on his shorts. Other men are similarly finishing their business, wiping their hands on kerchiefs, leaving. Intermission is almost over, and the herd is beginning to thin.

The long-faced stranger appears like a spectre next to him. He also tries the faucets, even though it's clear they are dry. He reties his shoelaces, already immaculately tied. He loosens and tightens his belt. His proximity makes the boy's heart crimp strangely, because the man's eyes are locked on him, unblinking, and his expression is grim with purpose.

'Oy,' a familiar voice calls from around the corner. 'Where are you Piddlyass?'

'Washing my hands, Brother,' calls the boy back.

'What a fragrant place!' Cousin-Brother says as he lets loose his own torrent. 'Finished everything?' His voice is the loudest thing in the toilet, resonating within the sealed concrete and tile space.

'Yes.' The boy is surprised he's even managed to say this, for the long-faced man has reached out and squeezed the front of the boy's shorts, delicately, casually, using the jutting sinks as cover. The gesture, its unexpected intensity, makes the boy stiffen with surprise. A smell of sweat and something else, sour and pungent, reaches him from the man. An old instinct tells the boy he should break away, run to Cousin-Brother, but a new, braver part of him desires very much to stay.

'Bitch!' says Cousin-Brother around the corner. 'She was with the party crowd. All cool and casual. "I looked for you, Raju." He mocks her with his high-pitched tone. "Then Sandy and Babs showed up, and I didn't want to miss the picture." Acting so coy, while that Sandy bastard kept giving her the eye. Fuck! She can park her dark ass on that behenchod's face if that's what she wants.' He pauses, grunts.

While Cousin-Brother speaks, the man moves his hand from the front of the boy's shorts and into the boy's pocket. The boy glances at the man with shy curiosity, but the man is staring ahead, serious and intent. His fingers press and caress and knead, making it hard for the boy to breathe, drawing sensations that make the boy want to twist and push further into the relentless hand. The boy feels a new sharp engorgement between his legs, a tugging that's quickly unbearable. The man suddenly withdraws his hand, making the boy wince with distress, then guides the boy's much smaller hand into his own pocket.

Cousin-Brother continues: 'I told her, "Here's your ticket, Seema. I spent a fifty for it. Keep it as a token of my affection." She made long lashes at me: "Sorry, Raju, Sandy had VIP box seats." Sandy took out his wallet and tried to give me a fifty. I told him to give it to some charity.' He finishes peeing in silence, snorting a few times.

The boy hears the upset in Cousin-Brother's refrain, knows it's about Seema didi as it often is. But his attention is with the thing straining upwards against the fabric of the man's pocket, warm and substantial and throbbing. The size of it confuses the boy, until his thrill makes a place for it in his imagination. He thinks of the king elephant from his class movie, rearing up his powerful trunk.

The man leaves the boy's hand where it is and reaches for the boy's zipper, but another, closer *Oy!* from around the corner makes him wrench his hand away and step back. Cousin-Brother's face appears. He takes in the man, scowls for a second, then looks at the boy.

'Why are you standing there like a pussy?' he says, as the man almost collides with him in his hurry to leave.

'Nothing, Brother,' says the boy, his own voice hoarse and unfamiliar. 'I was washing my hands.' He feels the heat of his artless lie on his face.

'Where?' says Cousin-Brother in a scoffing way. 'In this five-star bathroom?'

The boy walks slowly towards Cousin-Brother. Cousin-Brother takes out a small, square pocket mirror with an attached comb. He gives himself a look over in the mirror and passes the comb through his hair a few times. When he's done he does not look satisfied.

'A messed up day from the start,' he mutters. The boy stays quiet, head down. It's the best thing to do when Cousin-Brother is in this mood.

In the second half both have trouble focusing on the film. For Cousin-Brother the theatre may as well be dark and silent. For the boy the screen flickers with a hundred thousand tiny lights. When he closes his eyes the lights remain.

Later, on the way home, Cousin-Brother pinches the boy's arm and twists his ears mercilessly. It is a muggy evening, the roads to their colony full of slush from overflowing drains and washed up garbage. The boy remembers how Cousin-Brother is nice sometimes, like when he takes him to the sweet stall with Seema didi, or when he lets him carry his pads and bat to the cricket pitch. He wishes he could be like that all the time.

About every dozen yards Cousin-Brother torments the boy. The boy cries out, or smiles and pleads for him to stop. As though this is no different from any other day of being picked on. As though he is still a soft little boy. His own small duplicity thrills him.

Walking next to Cousin Brother, the boy treads on two feet of air between the ground and his shoes. He remembers that delicious pressure just below his navel, the muscles tensing as tight as a closed fist, the waves of contraction down his thighs and up the centre of his body. He vows to find that sensation again, for he wants it more fiercely than anything he remembers. The boy knows he must keep it a secret, from Cousin-Brother, from the world, this longing that hadn't existed this morning, that now leaks out of him like sweat. In the screen of the boy's imagination, the bathroom scene replays over and over, the details in brown and sepia: the smell of the man; the grim pleasure on his face; his own surprise, the initial urge to flee, and then the urge to stay, and to push, push, push into that strange and calloused hand.

THE MARRYING KIND

Mary Anne Mohanraj

CHICAGO, 1980

'This isn't working.' Leilani didn't say the words out loud, not with Jared working so hard, so earnestly, his large hands caressing her skin, his mouth travelling the hills and valleys of her body. It would have seemed cruel, after what felt like hours of his diligent efforts to arouse her laggard interest. After the first few nights of passion, Leilani had found it difficult to match Jared's interest, his attentions. It wasn't his fault—he was a nice man, intelligent, well-read, attentive. He was exactly the kind of man she had thought she was looking for. And yet here they were in bed, and where there should have been a wet, urgent heat, there was nothing. Worse than nothing—a dry chill; Leilani was dry as a bone, dry as an old woman, and she was only thirty-four, too young to be this cold and dry.

Her mother would have warned her, Leilani was sure, if her mother were still speaking to her, if her mother could have ever spoken so frankly of such things. This was the price Leilani paid for not marrying as a respectable girl would, for being restless, being wild. Her mother, born in another land, another time, would say that her daughter had used herself up, and despite her sensible self, Leilani felt a brief flicker of fear in her heart that maybe it was so. Maybe she had been too wild, for too long.

Thirty-four now—she had had sixteen years of love, men and women, passion and pleasure and joy and heartbreak and picking herself up and trying again. Not being willing to settle for just a nice lover, a good man, a kind woman—no, Leilani had seen the sad marriage her parents had had, the compromises of it, the costs. Instead she had wanted it all, had wanted the thundercrash, the lightning strike that hit over and over and over again and told you that this one was worth fighting for. She had thought she had found it, more than once, but it had never quite worked out, and so here she was trying again, with Jared. Jared who was large and powerful and strong and even passionate, but always gentle with her, as if she were a flower that might be crushed under the weight of a pounding storm.

This wasn't working, and if she didn't have the heart to tell him so in bed, at least she could make the job easier for him, and quicker for her. So the next time Jared slid down in the dark room, down to lick his way along her thighs, her calves, down to suck her toes, Leilani licked her own fingers and swiftly, sneakily slid them inside her, a quick motion, as practised and familiar as scooping rice and curry neatly into her mouth. This, at least, hadn't worn out, not yet, and a few quick strokes in exactly the right place was enough to raise her heartbeat, to bring her breath heavy into the summer-heated room, and that was enough for Jared who came back up, and she almost wasn't quick enough moving her hand away, but he didn't catch her. Then he was inside her, and it was wet enough, good enough for now, though a part of her felt sick at having used a whore's trick on the man. He was a good man. He deserved better.

Afterwards, Leilani slipped out of bed, pulled on a thin cotton robe, left Jared sleeping. It was late, and they both had to get up early the next day for work. But she couldn't sleep on a night like tonight—it was thunderstorm weather, and they were overdue. The forecasters had been predicting a storm for weeks, but there had been nothing, nothing but the crackle in the air, the build-up that never quite discharged. It was driving her slowly mad. Leilani walked through the long dark hallway, down past the dining room, the kitchen, following the same path on the ancient wooden floorboards that she had walked every night for the last week, heading out onto the back porch, out to where she could finally press her flesh against the wood railing, tilt her head back, gaze up and up at the dark sky, heavy with clouds that refused to give up their moisture. Not a star in sight.

It was so dark out here. She lived on the third floor, the top floor of the brownstone, and she could barely make out the outlines of her neighbours' porches tonight. No one would see if she decided to touch herself here, to relieve the frustration that still coiled within her, that radiated out from her centre to the tips of her fingers, the tips of her toes. Leilani could let the robe slip to the ground, could, naked in the night, mark a path across her skin with rough nails, dig fingers into flesh, leave bruises. She could fuck herself hard, here on this porch for all the world to see, because no one would see, fuck herself to exhaustion and satisfaction, with Jared safely asleep, never needing to know.

But she wouldn't do that, of course, because despite all her wildness, she wasn't that kind of girl–or at least, she wasn't any more. Sixteen years ago, she had let her first lover make love to her on a rooftop. Afterwards, the world seemed full of possibilities, an adventure waiting in every open doorway. Leilani had hurled herself into love, opened her heart as wide as it could go. But there had been one failed affair after another, each one ending for a different reason, but always, heart-wrenchingly, ending. And with each one, Leilani became a little more careful, more cautious.

Until here she was with Jared, with no idea why she was with him. Leilani couldn't tell him what she wanted, what she needed, and she didn't think he could give it to her anyway. It was time, past time, to break things off and set him free.

Jared wanted to marry her. He had told her that the day they met, as she walked down 57th Street to the bookstore and passed him leaning against a tree, a burly black man with his head shaved, sharp in crisp white shirt and dark blue jeans. The kind of man her mother would cross the street to avoid. He whistled as she walked by. Leilani turned a little and smiled, appreciating the compliment, the lift to her spirits on a grey May morning, and he said, 'A girl as pretty as you *must* be married.' And she laughed, as much at being called a girl as anything else, here in Hyde Park, a campus town where pretty little eighteen-year-olds filled the tree-lined streets. She laughed, charmed, and shaken her head no. And he smiled a wide smile of perfect shining teeth, and said, 'I sure would like to marry you myself.' Leilani had thought he was joking.

Leilani hadn't said anything more to him that day, but she saw him again, a few days later, in the bookstore this time, two volumes of Tacitus tucked under one arm, and a third spread on the book-lined table before him. An English translation, not the original Latin, but still. He was so deep in concentration that he didn't even notice her walking past, and that had charmed her too, and made her ashamed that she had seen the rich ebony shade of his skin and assumed that he was—well, not quite her kind, not the university, the intellectual, type. Later, over thick cheeseburgers and a shared chocolate milkshake at the Medici, she would discover that in fact Jared wasn't a grad student or a professor, that he did work in the physical plant, supervising the grounds crew, that he read ancient history for pleasure, for fun. That made it all the worse, of course. Sometimes Leilani thought that she had gone to bed with him a week later more out of embarrassment than anything else.

She admitted that to him, the following night over dinner. Leilani had cooked, basmati rice and spicy chicken curry, sweet carrots and green beens with turmeric sauce. She wasn't much of a cook, so had had to start over three times on the chicken curry, burning the onions the first time, scorching the meat the second. Leilani had been ready to scream with frustration, but had instead started over again, determined to finally, finally get it right. She had wished she could cook Jared a feast, an apology for what she'd been thinking. Over dinner that night, she said, her eyes fixed on her half-eaten plate, the words falling awkward out of her mouth, 'That first day, when we met—I didn't expect you to be smart. And when you asked me out, the only reason I said yes was because of the way you looked. Big. Strong.' *Dark and dangerous.* She didn't quite have the nerve to say that last, but the rest was bad enough. Leilani bit her lip, waiting for him to get angry, to storm out. It was what she deserved.

But instead, Jared was quiet for a long moment. Then he said, 'Well, I suppose I didn't know much about you when I saw you walking down that street. I knew you had that long black hair, so silky smooth, and I wanted to swim in it, like swimming in the ocean, at night.' He reached out, across the table, took a few strands of her hair in his fingerstips and tugged them, gently, making her look up at him. His eyes were calm, thoughtful. 'I knew your skin was like sweet coffee with cream.' Jared smiled then, that smile that had captured her the day they met. Smiled and said, with a sweet lilt in his voice, a sudden deep down-home accent, 'But now that I know you a little, I surely do like you, Miss Leilani. And I think you like me too.'

And Leilani had laughed, charmed by his speech, and by him, and admitting that it was true, that she did like him, liked the way he talked, the way he walked. She liked that Jared called his mother every night, just for a few minutes, just to say hello. Leilani liked that he could beat her at chess, which none of her lovers ever had. She liked that he could cook like a demon, that he made her johnny cakes with sweet honey, and barbecued ribs so tender that the flesh fell right off them. She especially liked that Jared had eaten everything that she had cooked, never saying a word of complaint about the chicken that still, despite all her efforts, managed to taste more than a little burnt. He was a good man, the kind of man you fell in love with, the kind of man you married. There was no good reason to think that he might not be the man for her.

At first, the sex had been good too.

The first night she brought him upstairs to her bed, as she unbuttoned Jared's white shirt, uncovering solid muscle over layers of more muscle, Leilani felt like it was her birthday, Christmas, even her wedding day, all rolled up into one. Jared was the best present ever. Six feet tall and so strong that he could pick her up with one arm. Over a week of dinners, and alone in her bed after, she had closed her eyes and slid her hand under the covers, between her legs. She had made herself crazy with fantasies of just how he would take her, how he would lose control, would slam her down into the bed, would ravage her willing body. And at first, he had seemed ardent enough, had covered her in kisses, traced long, slow paths from mouth to collarbone, from breast to nipple and then eagerly down to the triangle between her thighs.

Leilani had been wet that night, had been hungry for him, had spread her legs and invited him in with no hesitation at all. And when she finally had him inside her that first night, when he began to move, sending shivers through her, Leilani had raked her nails down her back, bit the flesh of his shoulder hard. Jared didn't complain—he'd taken it, taken everything she could dish out—but he didn't reciprocate. That night had been good enough, but it had made her nervous. And as she'd feared, no matter what she did to him, that night or the ones that followed, he was unfailingly gentle with her. Jared whispered sweet words in her ear. He said softly, 'I could really love you, girl.' Or even, 'You're the kind of girl I'd like to marry.' And then he kissed her again, softly, on the lips. He kissed her with respect, and it made her want to scream.

Leilani told herself, 'Well, he just needs to get to know me better.' But the nights and weeks went by, and though she whispered, 'faster,' 'harder,' Jared didn't seem able to take the hint. She hadn't been able to just come right out and say, 'I need you to fuck me really hard.' So maybe it was her fault that it hadn't gotten better—it had gotten worse. Until now, here they were.

For the last few weeks, the best part of dating Jared hadn't been when they were alone together—it was when they were out. They walked to campus and Leilani defiantly held his hand, enjoying the covert glances and outright stares. They went to restaurants together; they cuddled close in movies. At the Reynolds Club, they ate lunch with her professor friends on his break—then after he'd kissed her and left, Leilani smiled mysteriously at their fevered questions. *What's he like? Is he really on the grounds crew? This isn't serious, is it? What will your parents say?*

That one did make her heart thump, though she wasn't about to show it. By now, her parents would have heard the news from someone; her sisters would have discussed it all in detail; her father the professor might even have seen them, walking around campus, holding hands. But her parents hadn't spoken to her in years, so unless Leilani asked her sisters, she needn't know what they were saying. Someday her parents might speak to her again. Maybe if she got married. Maybe even if she married Jared. Her parents were educated people—they might be furious at their daughter, ashamed of her, for flagrantly having sex outside of marriage, but they would never admit, even to themselves, that they didn't want her to marry a black man.

At least Jared's family was honest.

Jared had begged Leilani to go with him to his sister's birthday party; begged with words, with soft touches to the back of her neck, with wide, dark eyes, until she would have found it easier to kick a puppy than say no to him. So Leilani had put on a sleeveless white dress, modestly knee-length, had brushed out her hair until it shone, and at his request, wore it loose and long. She had let him drive her west, past the university, into the areas where the students weren't supposed to walk. When they got out of the car, he'd put out his arm and she had slipped a hand through it, so that they might parade up the front walk to his mother's neat little house, cheerful with a fresh coat of yellow paint.

Leilani had been on display, and that was to be expected—she was the new girlfriend. What she hadn't expected was the way the men looked at her, with more concentrated lust than she'd ever experienced, an honest intensity of desire. They said to her face, *Girl, you are fine! Do you have any sisters?* Leilani blushed and Jared grinned wide, showing bright white teeth, shepherding her around with a proprietary hand on the small of her back. She could have handled the men, but then there were the women. Jared's mother, polite but cold. Jared's sister Kesia, whose skin was even darker than Jared's, and who neatly managed, with a plateful of food and a cold lemonade, to avoid shaking her hand. When Leilani went to use the washroom, she emerged to overhear Kesia hissing to Jared, angry and low, *What, you couldn't get a white girl, so you settled for next best?* And fury rose in Leilani, fury rose and then died, smothered by the knowledge that if Jared had picked her to satisfy some tainted craving, she had done worse.

'What are you doing out here?' Jared leaned in the doorway, his voice low and rough, his body huge and dark and menacing—or it would be, if it were her fantasy. But she knew him too well for that. Leilani fought to keep the frustration from her voice as she said, 'I couldn't sleep. Go back to bed. No need for both of us to be tired tomorrow.'

'You should come inside—it's going to storm.'

'They keep saying that, but it never happens. It drives me crazy.'

He was quiet a long moment. Then said, 'Are you talking about the storm, or about us?'

She hadn't realized that he knew how frustrated she was. Leilani had underestimated him again, but she was too angry to be embarrassed this time. Not that she had any right to be angry at him—he hadn't done anything wrong. It wasn't his fault that he was just too nice. The kind of guy she should be with, not the kind she wanted.

'This isn't working for me. I'm sorry, Jared.' What else could she say? *It isn't you, it's me?* Hard for anyone to believe that, and not much comfort even if you did. At least she was ending it early, before anyone could get too hurt. It had only been a few weeks.

He was quiet for a long time. Then, finally, 'You're not giving us much of a chance.'

Leilani wrapped her arms around herself, not wanting to see the lostness in his eyes. Maybe she'd been fooling herself, about no one getting hurt. Maybe it was too late. Maybe it had been too late from that first day, when he said he'd like to marry her. She wasn't the marrying kind.

'I think it's better this way. I do.' It wasn't really about the sex. The sex was just a symptom. Jared was a sweet guy. But Leilani needed more than sweetness.

'Well, then.' Heavy acceptance in his voice, and she was glad he wasn't going to fight her on this. Wasn't she? 'Come inside at least. It's starting to rain.'

A fat drop hit her arm, hard. And then another, and another. In less than a minute, the sky had opened up with the suddenness that you only found in a summer thunderstorm, and the rain was pounding down, wind whipping it along, and she was already drenched.

Slamming into her skin, blinding her, washing away all kinds of dirt and darkness. Leilani felt her heart lift, her pulse speeding up, racing. The rain was talking to her, telling her what she needed to do. One last chance.

'You go ahead,' she said quietly. 'I want to stay out here. Just for a little while.'

'Your clothes are getting soaked!'

'Then I'll take them off,' Leilani said, fighting back the urge to laugh. It wouldn't be kind, laughing now. But oh, her body wanted to, and that had nothing to do with Jared, and everything to do with the rain, with the sharp crack of thunder, and the lightning that whited-out the sky a moment later. Leilani slipped out of her robe and let it fall to deck, leaning back now against the railing again, closing her eyes, letting the warm rain pound against her face, her breasts, her belly. It was a good body to give to the night. No longer as slim as when she was the girl who liked to run, but with an added lushness now, curves that flashed in the lightning and then disappeared again into darkness.

Were there neighbours watching the storm, safe behind their windows? Watching her? Leilani didn't care. Let them hide inside and watch. Ah, *there* was the rush, the excitement she'd been missing. There was the part of herself she had lost. Leilani lifted her hands, cupped her breasts, dug her fingers into flesh. Felt shivers race beneath her skin as she squeezed her nipples between her fingertips. Was he watching? If Jared could walk away from *this*, then she'd know she was right to send him away.

'Damn, you're crazy, girl.' Finality in his voice, and the screen door slamming, and silence after. *Ah well,* Leilani thought. She'd tried her best. Maybe her best wasn't what Jared wanted. It hurt, but the pain slid into the hard wet wood against her back, the water-logged tendrils of her hair whipping in the wind, the slick trail her fingers followed down her body, down her belly, to that promised land she had lost sight of.

And then the door slammed back again, and Jared was there, one big hand grabbing her wrists, pulling them up, hard, above her head, to press against a post. The other hand on her flesh, hard and rough, not bothering with soft touches, long lingerings. Straight between her thighs, pressing her legs apart, shoving fingers up, inside, and god, she was wet. A few quick strokes and then Jared's hand was gone, leaving an aching emptiness; her hips arched up, involuntary, and thank god, thank god he was there to meet her. Naked as well, soaking wet and completely hard, his hand on her ass, lifting her up and onto him, so that her legs wrapped around him as far as they could go. Her hands still high above her head, her wrists still crushed in his grip, and it hurt, but that just made it better. He fucked her hard against the post, no gentleness left in him. She was racing now, racing the storm, and the storm was going to win, but that was fine, that was great. The lightning flashed, the thunder crashed, and she whited out in a shock that ran from head to toes to fingertips.

Afterwards, they lay together on the deck as the storm dwindled down, down to a few warm raindrops, here and there. Jared was solid beside her, warm. Her wrists ached, and so did other parts. Lots of other parts. There might be splinters in her back.

Jared rolled away, and for a chilly moment Leilani thought that he was going to get up, going to walk away, disgusted with them both, leaving her a used, crumpled heap on the wooden deck. There was always that possibility. A necessary risk. But he just rolled far enough away to raise up on one elbow, his thigh still pressed warm against hers, his dark eyes looking down at her. Smiling. Jared asked her then, his voice rough with what might have been anger, or passion, or laughter, 'So was *that* enough to satisfy you, girl?'

Leilani just smiled back, not sure of her answer. She reached up and pulled him down into a kiss. The storm was over, but there were many hours left until morning. *Maybe*, Leilani thought, her heart still pounding, her throat dry, *or maybe not.*

THE MONK

Ananda Devi

The monastery is built on the highest peak, well beyond the eye's reach. It is hidden behind deep clouds that, at this altitude, have a crystallized, shimmery texture. The way up is difficult to find and treacherous. No one can go up without a guide. And even the guides are sometimes reluctant to fetch anyone from the valley, as the steadiest feet can slip when the weather is wet, and the keenest eye can miss a fork—which means plummeting to death in the agony of utter silence.

They cannot speak, those who live here. They have made a vow of silence. They have also made numerous other vows. Poverty, humility, frugality and fasting, work, prayer, chastity. A denial of all of the body's desires. Hunger is fought with more hunger. Thirst with more thirst. Tiredness with more work. Pain with more pain. Cold with more cold. Silence with more silence. And so on. But perhaps for many of the young men who live here among the children and the elderly, the most difficult test is not ignoring desire, but erasing it altogether.

The nights are hard. They are alone in their tiny cells. Alone with stone walls, windows that open onto an impossibly sparkling night, the utter, pure silence of a tomb, and their thoughts. How do you quell the thoughts that no one hears? How do you prevent your body from reacting to them? The boys who came here as children have learned many things, but nothing surprises them more than the curious reaction of their body after puberty. They have known no women except their mothers and sisters, and they have no real knowledge of their shapes and secrets. And yet, when they are twelve or thirteen, they begin to see. They begin to imagine. How their mother or sister had twin swellings on the upper body that looked both soft and welcoming. How they had glimpsed their sister naked once, and it didn't mean anything then, but now fills them with surprise and sorrow, as they remember the roundedness and foreignness of the shapes that met their eyes. How they heard, as they waited to use the latrine, the musical tinkling of females passing water, so different from the harsh cascade of manly piss. How in the market places there were so many different types of women, so many different shapes and sizes, laughter and voices, and a kind of earthiness they hadn't noticed then but remember so well now, so clearly, because it is immeasurably distant from their way of life in the monastery; so different from who they are or are supposed to be, yearning for the ethereal and the spiritual as if their body must strive to disappear even before its death.

However much they struggle to repel the thoughts, the dreams are impossible to control. When they sleep, instead of the innocuous scenes that the childhood subconscious creates, strange delights are conjured. Their hands slide on elastic forms, stutter on improbable curves, their fingers explore dark, moist cavities, their mouths are filled with a savoury saliva, their tongue tastes the salt of sweaty skin, and their sex ... Their sex rears up with a savage longing, and in their dreams it has no bounds, it pushes and thrusts and pierces and penetrates, nothing stops it until it has released the warm, gel-like liquid that they have never seen until now, until they wake up and feel its stickiness on their thighs and belly and shamefacedly clean it in the freezing night so that the morning will bear no trace of it, save for a slight, but persistent scent that they hope no one will notice.

They cannot ask anyone about this. All are silent. Their eyes sometimes speak to another of their age, when some of the shame slips into their gaze and betrays them. But even though they suspect the other has shared the same experience, they have no answers. No one explains to them the mechanisms of the body, nor the natural needs for which it was created.

And so, they fast and they hunger and they work and they ponder, all the time feeling the eyes of the older monks upon them, cold, watchful and unforgiving.

He is seventeen years old. His name is Ananda. As soon as he could speak, he told his parents he was a monk.

He remembers his past life, he tells them. He needs to get back to the monastery. He remains a strict vegetarian and refuses any gifts, preferring to beg for his food. He spends hours without speaking, sitting in a corner of their humble house, eyes fixed on an unseen image.

He is indifferent to his parents' calls and entreaties. They do not know what to make of this child of theirs, so eagerly awaited, and so strange when he finally came. They feel somewhat short-changed, for they need a helping hand and a son to bear some of their burden: they do not need a saint. But in the end, they have no choice: when he is four years old, they agree to let him go to the monastery.

The same day, a monk clad in orange comes to their house. They try to hide their surprise, as they haven't told anyone about the child's request. Ananda greets the monk as a long lost friend, holding out his arms, but the monk looks at him coldly and gestures to him to follow. They leave immediately. For once, Ananda looks a bit lost. He glances back at his parents standing, desolate, in front of their house. A shadow fills his eyes and his face falls, as if his certainties have briefly wavered. But the monk tugs him roughly by his shirt and he turns away. His parents will never see their son again.

He follows the monk for long miles, gritting his teeth when his small legs threaten to collapse. He shows his resilience then, walking, sleeping on the ground, climbing with very little food and rest. He keeps waiting for the monk to praise him, but the monk never speaks and never smiles. He hardly looks at him. It takes a few days for Ananda to realize that the monk doesn't eat any of the food they've begged for but gives it all to the boy. The monk has gone without food since the first day they met. Ananda then stops eating all the food and leaves half of it behind. The monk thaws a little, giving him a slightly kinder look when his feet bleed on the harsh roads.

The climb to the monastery is an almost impossible ordeal. Never has the seemingly imperturbable child been so frightened before. He grits his teeth to prevent his fear or tears from showing. He no longer sees the monk clearly: the mist keeps changing shape as if on purpose to hide him, except for an occasional glimpse of orange that he holds on to when he thinks he is utterly lost. Rocks roll away under his feet, nearly toppling him over. He clings to the sides of the mountain with his small hands until he has clawed his nails bloody. His clothes are in tatters and he is shaking with cold. He wishes for the mist to clear, but when it finally does so, the vertiginous sight that meets his eyes is so terrifying that he freezes for long minutes, clinging to the cliff, until the monk beckons him on. He follows, step by painful step, persuaded that soon there will be no ground under his feet and the void will swallow him.

Ananda quickly gets used to the life at the monastery. He does not complain, even by a gesture or a sigh. He does all his chores and more. He fasts longer than is required for his age. He wants to be noticed, and he is. Some signs pass between the head monks, and he begins to see that they do indeed communicate, even without words. A hand occasionally corrects his movements with more gentleness than he is used to. When his writing of a sloka is particularly beautiful, he catches an almost imperceptible smile on the face of the manuscript master that he holds on to and treasures in his mind. The years pass by. His progress is astounding. Perhaps the masters begin to believe he is indeed the reincarnation of a monk who passed away years before. There is a shift—a kind of unspoken respect in the bodies around him. A space created just for him.

Until the night when the dreams begin.

Of course, Ananda doesn't know he is a boy like any other—in body, if not in mind. But because he has come here so young, he has no memories, like the other boys, of the mystery of the female body. He has no sisters, and his mother is now a distant memory, faded and fleshless. He has rarely seen other women. To him, the biological changes he's going through are unexpected and mysterious. He thinks he is possessed by a demon. He tries to fight the demon alone. He slowly succeeds in controlling his thoughts. But the dreams ...

Ah, the dreams are something else entirely. How can he let go of the slippery sweetness, the salty softness, the dark, the warmth, the trembling and the dizziness? How can he stop himself from dreaming of the curves and the lips? The eyes and the buttocks? The hips and the nipples? The dreams bring images that he has never seen and cannot understand. He still believes they are demons, but as the nights drag on, he begins to give in to their seductiveness. They chisel away at his resolve, taking over his body in glorious bursts of sensations. During the day, as he goes through his chores and duties, he thinks only of the night. He waits with a trembling awareness for the moment when he will fall into a deep sleep and lose all control.

He is not responsible for his dreams. That's what he tells himself when he wakes up and cleans his body in ice cold water. I am not responsible for my dreams. They may come to me, but I am still living a pure life, they cannot touch me or soil me.

But he cannot really hang on to this pretence. He knows he is surrendering to a terrible seduction, to some garden of fleshly delights that is totally contrary to what they are being taught here. His pleasure in the dreams is very far from the renunciation of all bodily needs that they must strive for.

He tries harder to forget. He puts himself through horrendous ordeals. He stops eating altogether, becoming but a shadow of himself. He goes for days without drinking any water, until his lips are blue and chapped, and his skin looks charred by the fever that begins to grow inside his starved flesh. He tries to go without sleep and does all the chores himself, cleaning the stone floors of the enormous monastery, washing the monks' bowls, washing their robes in icy water until his hands are raw and swollen.

But the older monks give him harsh looks and one morning send him back to his cell with a bowl of food and a cup of water. One of them stands over him until he eats, his hands shaking as if he were palsied, and until he sips his water little by little. The monk gestures that he must sleep. He tries weakly to protest, but the monk stands firm and he is too weak to fight. He settles down on the mat and immediately falls asleep.

Is it the deprivation and hunger? As soon as he sleeps, colours burst into his eyes. He is in a palace of silks. He is surrounded by fabrics of glorious colours, the blue of winter sun, the green of butterfly shadow, the yellow of bird nest, the violet of wet earth, and they flow of their own volition like water without a breeze. They sweep over him and past him, they slide in his armpits and between his thighs, they settle on his lips and over his eyes until every part of him is receiving silky caresses that awaken another type of fever from a point in his abdomen, radiating out. He rolls among the silks, but he knows he is waiting for something else. For someone else.

And then she comes, silent, naked, dark. She puts her finger on her lips: shhhh ... she says.

He hears it clearly: the whisper of an unknown voice: shhhh...

And a tinkle.

And a breath.

He opens his eyes. A woman is there. She smiles, her finger still on her mouth. She lies down next to him, doing nothing. He doesn't know what she is doing here, or even how she arrived. He looks at her naked body. She is only adorned with two bracelets that chime softly. Her hair is long and loose. She is as fleshy as he is skinny, as well-nourished as he is sickly. He raises his hand and touches the skin on her belly, suddenly dizzy with the warmth that rises from her. Her flesh is firm, her skin slightly moist with sweat. She guides his hand upwards and places it over her breast. He touches the large, dark nipples, exploring like a child the rubbery texture, feeling them harden under his palm. She sighs, looks at him with a smile and opens her mouth. He moves towards her, kisses her, first with his lips, then, wonderingly, with his tongue inside her mouth. He tastes cinnamon and aniseed on her tongue, and the memory of some sweet liquor that he has never drunk.

She slides the tips of her fingers over his back. Her nails softly graze his buttocks. He is thin, so thin there is almost nothing between his skin and his bones, and it feels as if she is touching him inside, as if her fingers have slipped under his skin and are awakening his blood. It flows, hot, inside his veins and arteries.

She then touches his sex, and the reaction is immediate. He is dazed by its power and effulgence, and by its dark, violet-tipped hunger. But she removes her hand quickly, shaking her head with a smile. He hears himself moan. He realizes that it is the first time he has heard his own voice in thirteen years. He wonders if it means he has broken his vows. Even coughs and sneezes must be smothered here. She puts her finger on his lips. Shhhh ... she says. It's both an order and a consolation.

He pulls her hand, wanting it back on his sex. But she resists. She sits up, pulls her hair over her shoulder and spreads it out over his face. Slowly, softly, her hair slides against his face, his mouth, his neck, his torso, then lower down over his sex, his thighs, his soles. He is nearly crying with desire. He looks at her and feels that the world has stopped. Nothing has ever seemed more beautiful to his eyes. She may be the charmer, the seducer, the serpent, the demon, but for such beauty he is ready to accept the burden of sin. To have seen such beauty is to have seen heaven, he thinks. So what if I must return to earthly pain for eternity? I will have this memory to tell me I indeed lived, once.

As she moves over him and at long last allows his sex to slip into hers, as she slowly lowers herself so that he moves deep inside the narrow, wet, warm and elastic cavity, he hears music building up inside him, some kind of unknown song, which he knows instinctively is the song of pleasure.

Her movements over him are a tortuous dance to which he sings silently, singing with her, inside her, until he comes and everything goes dark.

In the morning, Ananda sees the light coming through the window and the colour of the sky as if his eyes have opened for the first time. He kneels in front of the window and lets the cold wind touch his face and skin. He hears a running brook far away. He sees a distant bird flying lazily and gracefully. His hands touch the stone, worn smooth where he has sat for hours meditating. But now he thinks it is as smooth as a woman's skin.

Even in his cell, all this time, there have been wonders to see and feel, he thinks. But his whole life has been a denial of life. He looks down at this sad body, shrunken by fasting. His greyish skin, mottled by chastisement. The ugliness of his jutting bones. He remembers the creamy smoothness of his skin, as a child, and how his mother used to tell him he was beautiful. He wondered if that was what they did here, in the monastery: instead of glorifying creation, they rejected and refused it by shutting out and destroying all beauty, all wonder, all pleasure.

All they see are shaven heads, still eyes and faces, shapeless robes over shapeless bodies, and no song, no colour, no music, no smiles. Is that the price of heaven, he asks.

As he thinks about this, his mind is suddenly made up: I want to live, he says aloud.

Immediately, a group of monks come to his cell. They look at him with a rare anger, their eyes blazing. They've brought stones and cement, basins and trowels, and they wall up the window. They place a thick wooden door in the opening of his cell, which they bar from outside. When they are done, he is in complete darkness.

He smiles and lies down on his mat. He closes his eyes and sinks into his dream. The woman visits him again, as he expected. He has the feeling she is not part of the dream but a real person who manages to come into his cell by some hidden passageway. In the dark, he cannot see her, but she teaches him to see with his hands, to use his sense of smell and taste to know her better. He tremblingly tastes the substance that lines her vagina, and it tastes like nothing he has known before. He cannot describe it, since it is neither sweet nor salty, neither bitter nor acidic, but something else altogether—something he can only define as the taste of pleasure, just as he discovered the music of pleasure the night before. He tastes and tastes again, telling her he wants to carve this memory into his brain. She laughs until she cannot bear it anymore and comes with long, sinuous shudders in her body, and deep groans in her throat.

In turn, she takes him in her mouth and her tongue playfully laps the soft underside of his sex. You taste of sadness, she says when he comes. Her hands on his body show him how emaciated he is, how ugly his body has become. She cries silently. He feels her tears and licks them. It's as if an ocean of sorrow is filling me, he tells her. But then she laughs again, saying that she cries so seldom her tears would not fill his water cup. Her laughter dispels the sorrow.

The next day, he worries that his bodily functions, albeit rarer because of his constant fasting, will disgust her with their smell. He waits for sleep to come, but the worrying keeps it at bay. He knows that, as long as he doesn't sleep, she will not come. He tries to clear his mind and meditate, but this seems like treason, both against her and the monks. So he lies there and waits, sometimes hearing the distant noises of the monastery, a clanging outside time, but mostly hearing nothing, nothing at all, not even the pleasure song in his body.

At last, exhausted, he sleeps. She appears. He immediately asks her about the smell. She says there is no shame. Shame? He asks. What you have learned here is mostly about shame, she answers. You are even ashamed to laugh. Soon you will be ashamed to breathe. What is the point of living if you strive to be as a corpse, without feeling?

That's the way we communicate with the higher spirit, he says.

She shakes her head. You were created as a whole. You cannot separate your mind from your body, your emotions from your intellect, life from love. If there is no love, there is no living.

He thinks about their life in the monastery, and the harshness or indifference of the monks, and he suddenly remembers how his parents have doted on him and how he has rejected them with disdain. My parents loved me, he says.

They love you still, she replies.

And you? He asks timidly.

Do you reach the higher spirit quickly? She asks, a hint of mockery in her voice.

No, it takes years and years.

Then love also takes years and years. There are stages in love just as in prayer and meditation. You are learning the music and smell and taste of pleasure. There are other things to learn.

And so, every night, she teaches him. Never has he had a more beautiful teacher, nor more wonderful lessons. She lies on her belly and makes him touch the powerful arcs of her buttocks and the pungent darkness in between. She shows him there are other, hidden ways inside her, with his fingers, his tongue, his sex. She teaches him to accept and to inflict some pain that swiftly moves to an altogether different sensation, although their shouts seem to express both pain and hunger. A different pain, a different hunger, a different thirst from those he knew before, because now they will burst into a pulsating, vibrant, piercingly beautiful effusion of their bodies. Before, they only led to a slow death. Now they are the openings of life.

She teaches him to delay his orgasm until they have explored all these possibilities and brought themselves to a state of near-frenzy. He learns the places that arouse her most. He also learns the endless games they can play, how they can tease each other until they are laughing one minute and almost crying with need the next.

He begins to realize that the body is a door. It leads to other discoveries. And that knowing her body does not mean he knows her. On the contrary, her inner self remains a mystery, shrouded in wonderfully coloured silks, unseen and unfathomable.

One day, she says: you cannot really fast if you haven't tasted food. It's when you know all the tastes and the textures that you can relinquish them without regret.

And so she brings to his cell the most delicate and elaborate food, in small warm copper bowls. He sits and eats in the dark, slowly, tasting every morsel and learning to understand the taste before swallowing and passing on to the next morsel. Sweet salty bitter acidic, she says teasingly. Nothing like your taste, he answers with a smile.

Every delicacy is like a trip into the unknown, for all his life he has eaten the blandest and stingiest of food. Even paupers occasionally taste something good, she says. You deny yourselves everything. She also brings some liquor and only allows him to taste a drop, because he is so weak and thin, more would kill him. He listens to the warmth coursing through his body, but then says that the headiness of love-making is far better than the one brought on by liquor.

The endless varieties of sweets, tasting of rose and coconut and mango and cinnamon, take him by surprise. She places tiny morsels on her supine body and he finds them in the dark. They are both sticky and glutted, tasting of cooked cream and pistachio, mashed mango and rose syrup. They lie together, his finger moving softly inside her, the memory of the different tastes continues to burst in his mind like tiny epiphanies.

Days pass and the monks do not come back. They do not feed Ananda. They do not clean his cell. It's as if they've forgotten all about him. He doesn't care. He is being fed. More than enough. He laughs aloud at their sad lives, the chores, the penance, the greyness of it all, when there is such a rich and wondrous world to be discovered. He thinks he is putting on weight, ripening into a warm-blooded young man, ready to serve his love with all the knowledge that she has been giving him.

She brings him an instrument and he plays and sings songs about life and love and colours and silks and pleasure and laughter. The monastery shakes with the sudden, unfamiliar noise. The other monks stop and listen. The younger ones realize that he is singing about their silent yearnings. Tears come to their eyes as they begin to understand each note and each verse. They sing to themselves silently before they go to sleep, and the songs seep into their dreams, bringing their own images and fantasies.

The next day, the monks open up Ananda's cell, take him out and down long staircases, some of which have not been trodden for centuries. Down, down, down, and through long passageways and tunnels that run through the mountain to buried caves that only the monks know of, deep in the belly of the earth.

They put him in a cave, with some food and water to last a few days. Their eyes are full of regret instead of fury. One of them kneels and begs for his forgiveness.

Surprised, he raises his hand in blessing. And then he realizes that they are walling up the opening through which they came. They are sealing the cave. He will be left here, alone with himself, and will live until the food lasts and his body survives. He understands that they will not come back for him.

The stone door rises slowly. Higher and higher. In the end, he only sees the eyes of the monks. One of them looks at him, and slides a sharp, metal tool inside the cave just before closing the last gap. Ananda picks the tool up, knowing his only way out is through death.

He waits, but she doesn't come. He sleeps, but he only dreams, he knows that she hasn't really been with him. He sings, but the utter silence swallows his voice. He is alone.

He cries then, and shouts and hits the walls, anger swelling inside him as he thinks of the treacherousness of them all—the monks and the woman. Of his young life cut short in this horrible way.

Why me, he asks. He doesn't know who to call. The monks will not answer. The higher spirit will not answer. The old gods will not answer. And the woman will not answer. He doesn't even know her name.

Why doesn't she come now, when he most needs her?

He rants and raves and falls into a deep, haunted sleep, wakes up, rants, raves, and on and on.

Why won't she come?

And then he remembers what she said about food. It's only when you've tasted it all that you know the meaning of fasting.

One day, his hand finds the metal tool left behind. He picks it up, looks at the dark surrounding him, and breathes a sigh of relief as he realizes that he can end it all.

As his hand tightens on the tool and starts to rise to his throat, he remembers the woman. He recalls her with a perfect vision—not just vision but smell, touch and taste. He realizes that his body has kept both her imprint and her mystery. And that both are as precious to him as every moment he has shared with her. She gave herself to me, he thinks. And the words have a different meaning. An absolute, fabulous gift he nearly missed in his misery.

He starts to carve a small figure in the stone wall, using his hands and his senses to guide him. He carves her smells, and her tastes, and her touch and her voice.

Time passes. He forgets that the tool would have given him an easy death. He keeps on carving and sculpting her, even though his food and water have long gone, and his robe is in tatters, and in the dark he looks more like a skeleton than a man. Still, he has more to show. He won't stop. (She's taught him how to delay, how to keep going, how to prepare for the long awaited eruption.) The metal tool wears down to a useless shred and he starts to carve the walls with his own nails. The cave is immense. His fingers keep finding more empty spaces and his mind more images of her. When his nails wear out, he uses his knuckles, then his bones. His blood stains the stone a deeper black.

At last he knows she is all there, all of her. Her face and breasts and belly and thighs and buttocks and hair. His flesh and bones are there too: his mouth has bled into hers, his tongue has rasped itself thin on her tongue, her hair is mixed with his own, grown long and soft, his teeth remain around her wrists and ankles like the jewels she wore, and his sex has slowly, softly, dug into the stone the exact shape of her vagina.

When he dies, he is deep inside her, melted and merged with her, knowing he has recreated her with everything he has and is, his own bones and fluids and flesh, with his own life-source, a pleasure that should never be denied.

NEXT YEAR AT THE TAJ

Sheba Karim

Rahul had seen a girl at a bar in Connaught Place who'd reminded him of Nandini before, wide hips, throaty laugh, thick, spiral curls. The girl leaned over to pick up a pack of cigarettes that had fallen to the floor, and Rahul thought of how he used to love to fuck Nandini like that, her hands braced against the wall, her round ass pumping against him. That night he was so horny that, against his better judgment, he reached for Nandini across the bed, only to have her recoil.

'Please, Nandini,' he said.

'That's all you care about, isn't it?' she said. 'Unbelievable, Rahul. You don't need a wife, you need a whore.'

It was unfair, but then Nandini was often unfair these days. She switched off the lamp and turned away and Rahul watched the shadows of the siri tree's long, phallic fruit pods move along the wall, rustled by the wind. His balls ached. His heart did, too. Last week, Nandini had said, 'I wish I'd never told them.' He'd understood right away what she meant—the night her father had called at 2 a.m. and without thinking he'd picked up her phone. 'Kaun hai?' her father had demanded. Rahul panicked and hung up, and Nandini decided she'd tell her parents about him. Her parents had called his parents. Our daughter is a respectable girl from a respectable family. If your son is serious about her, he should marry her. And if he's not serious about her, then what is he doing? And so they'd gotten married, which was fine because Rahul had loved her. He still loved her, the old Nandini at least, not this stranger who had stopped looking for a job, spent half the day stoned, obsessively watered the plants and then cried when one died, who'd gone to see a past-life regressionist and told Rahul that she'd once been a long-suffering widow but refused to elaborate further because, she said, he'd never understand.

All along he'd been patient. It was the miscarriage, he'd told himself, but months went by, then a year, Nandini withdrawing more and more, until she stopped touching him completely.

Nandini whimpered into her pillow. Rahul put his arm around her, and the pressure of her ass against him made him hard again. He didn't dare jerk off next to her, so he waited until she sighed softly and fell into a better dream before going to the bathroom. Sitting on the toilet lid, his worn boxers around his ankles, he gripped his cock and remembered. The terrace of Nandini's old barsati, late night, bleached purple sky. They'd come back a little drunk from a photography opening, back when he still dreamed of having his own work on a gallery wall. They smoked a joint on her terrace. She was wearing a short green summer dress and telling him a story about a childhood trip to Mount Abu. The story involved a nasty fight between her parents, but he couldn't help getting hard, because she wasn't wearing underwear and as she talked her legs fell open and closed, open and closed. By the third glimpse, he couldn't take it anymore. He got on the ground and pushed her knees apart and started licking the tender skin of her inner thigh as Nandini gasped in surprise. He made love to her cunt that night, licking her slowly, gently, in, out, around, the length of her lips, the tender stretch of her perineum, and by the time he got to her clit she was wet and trembling, and the orgasm clenched inside her released so powerfully that her entire body quaked, cum gushing out of her, and she wept a little. He kissed her slick thighs until she was still again, then lifted his head, his chin dripping in her juice, his cock insanely hard, proud that he'd just made a beautiful woman come like this. 'Sundari,' he said. A street dog howled and a chaukidar blew his shrill whistle and she pulled off her dress, leaned back in the bamboo chair and spread her legs wide, ready for him. As Rahul entered her, he thanked God for this, for his sundari Nandini, naked on the terrace, smiling with him with such love in her eyes.

Rahul wiped the cum off his stomach with toilet paper. As much as this memory gave him hope that if they'd loved like that once, they could again, it also reminded him how much they'd lost, first a baby, then each other.

They hadn't had sex in more than a year. Seeing that girl at the bar had made him realize how desperately he needed to be touched. You want a whore, Nandini had said. He was going to New York for work next week. Maybe it wasn't a bad idea.

Last night in New York. Client dinner cancelled. None of his friends in the city knew he was here. Nandini wouldn't call; she never did, anymore. There would be no better time to use the number than this.

Sunil had given him the number two years ago, before his first business trip to New York. 'It'll cost you, but she'll be worth it,' he'd told him. He remembered feeling sorry for Sunil then, that while Nandini wanted to fuck him every day, Sunil had to pay whores for sex. But he'd kept the number anyway, in an inner pocket of his laptop bag. He'd been staring at the yellow slip of paper for the past half hour, making tiny rips all around it. What had someone told him once? To make rips like that meant you were sexually frustrated.

Well, wasn't he? How had it come to this? When did the most erotic part of his life become his memories?

Just this once. Anonymous hotel room, anonymous woman. He'd never even know her real name. He deserved it. It wouldn't hurt anyone.

Fuck it.

He picked up his mobile and dialled, thinking perhaps the number had changed. These types of places probably changed numbers every few months.

'Elite Encounters. How can I help you?'

'Hello. I'm calling because ...' he tried to remember what Sunil had told him. Do not say whore, or hooker, or sex. 'I'd like an escort for this evening.'

'Have you used our service before?'

'No.'

'Well, we pride ourselves in having escorts who are beautiful, intelligent and classy, and we offer full female companionship.'

Full female companionship. That had to be a euphemism for sex.

'Sir? Are you there?'

'Yes. Yes, that sounds good.'

'Excellent,' the woman said. 'Let me explain our charges. There's an agency fee of a hundred dollars, and a cash tip for the escort.'

'And how much would that be?'

'It's a four hundred dollar tip per hour.'

Four hundred dollars. Plus a hundred dollar fee. Five hundred dollars for one hour. More than twenty thousand rupees. He had thirty dollars and five hundred rupees in his wallet. 'One hour would be fine.'

'And what time would you like your escort to meet you?'

He glanced at the clock. 6:48 p.m. 'Eight?'

'Let me check our availability.' She put him on hold. Rahul told himself, this is it, last chance to hang up, walk away, but he kept the phone tightly pressed to his ear. 'I have three escorts available at that time. The first is Pepper, she's 5′11″, 36-24-34, reddish-brown hair, the cheerleader type, busty but athletic. Does that sound like something you'd be interested in?'

'Uh ...' He pictured a busty blonde towering over him with blue and white pom poms. 'Maybe?'

'Why don't you tell me what you're looking for? That way I can see which one best suits your needs.'

What the hell was he looking for? A Nandini with love in her eyes? That would not be an option. 'Do you have anyone average height, with long, curly hair and ... not too large a chest?'

'Yes, I have Marissa. Marissa is 5′6″, long, curly blonde hair, brown eyes.'

'I'll take her,' he said.

Rahul was starving and wanted to order the bacon cheeseburger from room service but, thinking that this was a bad idea given tonight's activities, got an Asian noodle salad instead. He watched TV while he ate. The host of some entertainment show was talking about the fabulous wedding of a divorced celebrity couple who were remarrying each other. 'Here's to happily ever after, again!' the host chimed cheerfully.

Whoever was staying a few rooms down had hung a 'Do Not Disturb Sign' on their door. Their room service tray was outside, an empty bottle of champagne in a silver ice bucket, two flutes, a rose petal lying on the white cloth. Rahul left his own tray, the half-eaten salad with wilting lettuce, next to it and checked his watch. 7:18. Time to get ready.

As he showered, he wondered what Nandini would say if she saw him now, in a hotel bathroom halfway across the world, soaping up his balls and crack for a whore.

Could it be any worse than what she'd said to him as he was leaving for the airport? 'I think we married too soon. I think we confused love with sex.'

He tried to jerk off in the shower so he'd last longer with Marissa 5′6″ but ended up examining the bulging vein on his cock instead. It looked like it'd gotten bigger. Maybe he should see the doctor. Maybe something was wrong. Could a cock have an aneurism?

Stop it. Your cock is fine. Everything is fine. You'll have a nice fuck and that will be the end of it. Nandini will ever know.

In her heels, Marissa was much taller than 5′6″, and Rahul was disappointed that she'd blow-dried her hair straight, but the rest of her was as described, blonde hair, dark brown eyes, high, freckled cheekbones, small but promising tits peeking out from her black dress. It was a striking combination, blonde hair and dark brown eyes.

'May I come in?' Marissa said.

He stepped aside. 'Yes. Yes. Please.'

Now that there was a hot woman standing in the narrow space between his bed and desk, his room seemed even smaller.

'They wouldn't let me upgrade,' he explained, though he hadn't even tried.

'Oh, that's all right.' She had a deep voice, with a slight rasp. It was exactly the kind of voice you'd expect from a woman of her profession, and he wondered if it was real. Marissa sat on the edge of the bed, leaning back a little, and Rahul's cock stirred at the sight of her dress inching up her thighs. He shifted his gaze to someplace safer. The bottoms of her black stiletto heels were blood red. Shit. That was definitely real.

'Have you used our service before?' she asked.

'No. This is my first time.' He cleared his throat, rubbed his sweaty palms on his pants. 'With any service.'

'Well, welcome!' she said, sounding so genuine that Rahul was about to thank her. 'Do you mind if I take a look at your passport?'

'Yes. I mean, no, I don't mind.' It took three fumbling tries to open the clasp of his laptop case. He must seem like an idiot. Or worse, a virgin.

'India!' she exclaimed when he handed her his passport. 'Neat. I've always wanted to go there.'

'You should. It's very nice,' he said. Nice. Could he not come up with a more compelling word?

She tossed her head so her hair fell back. A heart-shaped diamond sparkled between her freckled collarbones. 'I know it must sound touristy, but I've always wanted to visit the Taj Mahal. I've wanted to see it ever since I saw a picture of it in one of my sister's history books. I thought the whole story was so romantic. I used to dream of getting married there. I know, it must sound cheesy to you. But I still want to go. And I'm pretty sure I am going, next year.'

'You should. It is a little touristy, but it's beautiful. Though, actually, I've never been there,' he admitted.

'No? Why not?'

'Well, my parents took me when I was a baby, but I haven't been since. I do have a photo, though, of me in a stroller in front of it.'

She laughed, her leg brushing lightly against his. 'It must be cute.'

'Yeah, Nan—' He was about to say Nandini had liked it so much that she'd swiped it from his parents' photo album. Nandini. For the past five minutes, he'd completely forgotten about her. Somehow, that seemed like a worse betrayal than what he was about to do. 'Yes, it's pretty cute.'

'Well, then, Rahul, here's to next year at the Taj, for both of us,' she said, like a toast, and he realized he hadn't offered her anything.

'Would you like something to drink?'

'No, thank you. So, what do you do, Rahul?'

'I'm a management consultant.'

'That sounds interesting.'

'It's all right. I used to want to be a photographer.' Why was he telling her this?

'Why didn't you become one?'

'There's no money in it, I guess.'

'Do you still photograph?'

'Not anymore.'

'Why not?'

Because, a few weeks after the miscarriage, Nandini and he had gotten into a fight. She'd called him an emotional cripple, and then she'd said, 'And your photographs are unimaginative and pedestrian.' After that, he'd never been able to pick up his camera again.

Marissa was looking at him. She gave him a warm smile. 'Well, I hope you take it up again, because I'm sure you're very talented. So, how about we get started?'

'Sure.' He hadn't felt this excited since the first time he'd had sex with Nandini without a condom.

'Great! So I do need to take care of some business first,' she said apologetically. 'I'm sure the agency explained that there's a hundred dollar agency fee. There's also a four hundred dollar per hour tip for my services. This includes one orgasm. If you want to come again, it'll be another two hundred dollars.'

Two hundred dollars. The world labour economies were so fucked up. Three maids for a month in Delhi, or a second orgasm in New York.

'All right,' he said.

'And what would you like to do, Rahul?' Raaa-hool, she pronounced it, with a little rasp. 'Some clients want to come from a blow job, some from intercourse, some want the girlfriend experience, you know, kiss, cuddle, pillow talk. I'd love to do anything with you, except anal, bondage, that kind of stuff. I don't do that.'

Anal, bondage. The closest he'd gotten to anal was when he was once fucking Nandini from behind in the dark and mistaken her asshole for her vagina, and that had lasted about two seconds.

She stroked the length of his calf with the tip of her shoe, and his cock rose again. 'Don't worry—you can tell me. I'm here for you.' As sexy as she was, there was also something almost maternal about her, like you could fuck her and then cry in her arms.

Fuck her. That's how he wanted to come, and it was a bad idea to let her suck him, even for a minute; it'd been so long since a mouth was on his cock that he might just come right away, and then he couldn't afford to come again.

'I'd like to come from sex. Intercourse,' he said, forcing himself to look at her as he said it.

'Great.' She smiled wide, her teeth straight and gleaming white, like a toothpaste commercial. She paused, glanced around the room, and then smiled at him again, like she was waiting for something. 'The payment,' she said, gently.

'Sorry—it's on the nightstand.' That's another thing Sunil had told him. Never hand them the money. Leave it in an envelope, let her pick it up.

She walked the few steps to the nightstand and bent over. She had a nice ass, curvy like Nandini's. A good ass to squeeze while licking pussy. Would she let him do that too?

Marissa looked over her shoulder as if she'd heard the question, but she said, 'Do you mind if I use the bathroom for a moment?'

'No. No. Please.'

'Thanks. I'll just be a minute. Why don't you get more comfortable?'

The room was so small that the bathroom door practically hit the bed as she opened it. The clock flashed 8:15. 6:45 am in Delhi. Nandini would be fast asleep, her fist tucked under her chin.

He heard the water running, Marissa talking to someone on the phone.

Get more comfortable, she'd said. This meant undress. He stripped down. He'd forgotten about the hole in the crotch of his blue striped boxers. He crossed his legs, but that seemed gay, so he uncrossed them and put his hand there instead. The door opened, and he sat up straight, sucked in his stomach.

'Mind if I join you?' Marissa said. She looked like a model from a Victoria's Secret catalogue, black and maroon lacy bra, matching underwear, thigh-high black stockings with lace garters, one hand on her hip, high heels still on.

'Of course,' he said. She came next to him and he'd never seen legs so long, a stomach so flat. The skin between her lace-covered tits shimmered a little. He was trying to psyche himself up to make a move when she rested her hand on his thigh and squeezed it gently.

'Would you kiss me?' she said. 'I'd really like that.'

Would he remember how to kiss? Of course he would. It was like riding a bike. She was leaning in closer, and he closed his eyes and went for it, finding her cheek first, the minty freshness of her mouth, and then her tongue, and he finally began to relax, and as his tongue slid over hers he became confident as well, that not only could he do this, but do it well. He cupped one of her breasts and moaned at the soft weight of it. He undid her bra on the first try with one hand, a move he'd always been proud of, and began to suck on her tits, but, worried he might come just from her rosy nipples stiffening underneath his tongue, her little raspy grunts, he stopped, pulled away to catch his breath.

She used this pause to get naked, unhooking her garters, removing her hose one long leg at a time, taking off her underwear, and then lay before him. She had no dimples or stretch marks like Nandini, her perky tits and completely shaved crotch even paler than the rest of her, a spread of dark freckles below her belly button. She saw him looking and opened her legs, revealing the pink flaps of her cunt, and all he wanted to do was lick them, play with her clit as he kneaded her ass, feel her writhe and rasp and burst.

'What are you thinking?' she asked, her hand gliding down her body seductively, her nails the same red as the bottom of her shoes.

He swallowed. Say it. She's here for you, remember? 'I'm thinking I want to go down on you.'

'I can come great from sex, so you should only do it if it's what *you* really want.'

'It is.'

'Then, sure, Rahul,' she said. 'I'd love that.'

She spread her knees so wide that they were almost flush with the bed, but Rahul wanted to warm her up first. He kissed the freckles on her stomach, palmed her ass cheeks, licked the dark amoeba birthmark that went from her inner thigh to the edge of her cunt, tilted her upwards and licked those petal pink flaps. When he closed his eyes, the only things that distinguished her cunt from Nandini's were its lack of hair, the smell of talcum powder. She was very wet now, and saying fuck yes fuck yes. She shuddered as he pushed his tongue all the way inside her, and by the time he'd moved on to flicking the underside of her clit she was already saying 'I'm going to come' and he only had to move the tip of his tongue in a circle around the round tartness of her clit before her arched lower back began to tremor, waves of pleasure rising and falling beneath her skin, though she didn't squirt as he'd hoped. When it was over, he raised his head, about to say 'Sundari' like he always did, but he was between the legs of a stranger and his heart ached again. Then he saw her flushed cheeks and parted lips, her erect nipples and when she put her hand on his cock and said, 'Look at you,' he knew he'd die if he didn't fuck her this second. She reached into her purse and handed him a condom, played with her tits as he rolled it on. 'How do you want to fuck me?' she asked.

'Turn around,' he said.

She flipped over, stuck her ass in the air. His cock felt so huge in her hot, moist pussy that he knew he had to move nice and slow or he might come, but even nice and slow felt so fucking warm and tight he knew it was only a matter of time. Oh Raahool, she rasped, head thrown back, her blonde hair spilling over her ass. He grabbed her hips and started to pump into her hard. She pumped back, saying I'm going to come I'm going to come and as he reached for her tits her pussy gripped him harder and he came, the pleasure like a fist, moving down his cock, emptying inside her.

The sex couldn't have lasted more than a minute but Rahul felt so good he didn't care. With a deep sigh he sank onto the duvet, rested his head on her shoulder. She seemed to understand that he didn't want to speak, and lay quietly next to him, holding his hand. Strange, he thought, how you could find comfort in the arms of a total stranger. He closed his eyes and let himself drift. Nandini. Forgive me. It's you I want. Tomorrow he'd go back to Delhi and talk to her, he'd make it work, make it like it used to be. He'd take her to the Taj Mahal. They'd run into Marissa and her new husband, take a photo of the newlyweds, and then Marissa would take a photo of them. Yes. He could see it in the frame, Nandini inside

Rahul's arms, brilliant white dome against clear blue sky. Next year at the Taj. Nandini with love in her eyes. Happily ever after, again.

CONTRIBUTORS

Abeer Hoque is a Nigerian born Bangladeshi American writer and photographer. She also carries too many bags. See more at olivewitch.com.

Amitava Kumar is the author of several works of non-fiction and a novel. His latest book, *A Foreigner Carrying in the Crook of His Arm a Tiny Bomb*, was judged the 'Best Non-Fiction Book of the Year' at the Page Turner Literary Award. His debut novel, *Home Products*, was short-listed for the Vodafone Crossword Book Award. He is a Professor of English on the Helen D. Lockwood Chair at Vassar College in upstate New York.

Ananda Devi is one of the major French language writers from Mauritius and the Indian Ocean. She has won several international prizes and her novels, published by the French publisher Gallimard, have been translated into several languages. She received the title of 'Chevalier des Arts et des Lettres' from the French government in 2010. Her major novels are *Eve de Ses Décombres*, *Indian Tango* and *Le Sari Vert*.

Gudiya has two-and-a-half languages, and three silver scars on her pericardium.

Hansda Sowvendra Shekhar was born in 1983 in Ranchi and grew up in Ghatsila sub-division of Jharkhand, India. He is currently working on his first novel. His first novel, 'The Mysterious Ailment of Rupi Baskay', will be published in May 2013 by Aleph Book Company.

Lopa Ghosh has meandered through literature, journalism, street theatre, a London stint seeking causality and Sylvia Plath's house, severe delusion and serious feminism. Her short story collection, *Revolt of the Fish Eaters*, was published by HarperCollins in May 2012. Ghosh now lives and works in Delhi.

M. Svairini is the creatrix of The Bottom Runs the Fuck: Stories. She is the winner of a National Leather Association: International writing award and has contributed smut to *Safeword* magazine, literary zines, *Yoni Ki Baat* (a South Asian version of *The Vagina Monologues*), and the Circlet Press anthology *Up for Grabs 2: The Third Gender.* You can follow her slavishly on Twitter at @msvairini.

Mary Anne Mohanraj wrote 'Bodies in Motion' (a finalist for the Asian American Book Awards and translated into six languages), as well as nine other publications. She received a Breaking Barriers Award from the Chicago Foundation for Women for her work in Asian American arts organizing, and has also won an Illinois Arts Council Fellowship.

MOHAN SIKKA'S story 'Uncle Musto Takes a Mistress' was selected for a 2009 PEN/O. Henry Prize. His fiction has appeared in *One Story*, the *Toronto South Asian Review*, *Trikone Magazine*, and in magazines and anthologies in several countries. Mohan's story 'Railway Aunty' was published in *Delhi Noir*. It is being adapted into a feature film, entitled 'B.A. Pass', to be released in 2012.

SHEBA KARIM writes fiction for adults of all ages. Find out more at www.shebakarim.com.

SHRIMOYEE NANDINI is a some time lawyer, and fulltime student based in Delhi. She has been previously published in *Pratilipi*.

RABI THAPA'S debut collection of short stories, *Nothing to Declare*, was published in 2011. Previously the editor of the weekly *Nepali Times*, he is based in Kathmandu. He is an advisor to the annual Kathmandu Literary Jatra and is working on a novel about a journalist who goes mad.

RANBIR SIDHU is the author of *Good Indian Girls*, a collection of stories, and is a winner of the Pushcart Prize for fiction. His first novel will be published in 2013.

ACKNOWLEDGMENTS

The first acknowledgment must go to my wonderful and talented contributors, who have made this book what it is and who never complained when I asked for another round of revisions but graciously came back with a draft even better than I'd hoped.

My sincere thanks to Ledig House, Millay Colony for the Arts, Nicky Dodd and Sev and Ellen Fowles for offering such lovely spaces to think and write, my agent Ayesha Pande for her suggestions and support, Deepthi Talwar and all of the people at Tranquebar for allowing me this opportunity and making this anthology possible. And to Anand, who encouraged me to take on this project, and whose feedback, love and coffee were instrumental to this book's journey from notion to reality.